For Tina, Carly, and Kalyn,
who have taken their stand
against injustice

There's More Adventure in the CHRISTIAN HERITAGE SERIES!

The Salem Years, 1689–1691

The Rescue #1   *The Accused* #4
The Stowaway #2   *The Samaritan* #5
The Guardian #3   *The Secret* #6

The Williamsburg Years, 1780–1781

The Rebel #1   *The Prisoner* #4
The Thief #2   *The Invasion* #5
The Burden #3   *The Battle* #6

The Charleston Years, 1860–1861

The Misfit #1   *The Trap* #4
The Ally #2   *The Hostage* #5
The Threat #3   *The Escape* #6

The Chicago Years, 1928–1929

The Trick #1   *The Stunt* #4
The Chase #2   *The Caper* #5
The Capture #3   *The Pursuit* #6

The Santa Fe Years, 1944–1945

The Discovery #1   *The Stand* #3
The Mirage #2   *The Mission* #4

I don't wanna go back to school. School is dumb!"

Twelve-year-old Will Hutchinson paused over the boca-
dillo he was about to bite into and shook his head at Fawn, his
11-year-old foster sister. "It isn't *school* that's dumb," he said. "It's
all the junk we hadda do to get *ready* for school. Registration.
Vaccinations—"

Beside him, Abe soon-to-be-Kates rose up over his bowl of paella like a bear emerging from hibernation. "No more vaccines!"
he said, his big-cheeked face screaming-red. "You say no more
vaccines, Mutti!"

Abe made a panicked turn to Tina Kates, the petite woman
next to him, who put her hand on his big face and said, "No more
shots, Abe. We're all done with those."

Abe gave an immediate grin, as if there were no such *thing* as
vaccination shots, and dove back to his rice dish. Will shrugged at
the lady Abe had called Mutti, the German word for mother.
"Sorry, Mrs. Kates," he said. "I forgot he was scared of doctors and
stuff."

"How could you forget?" Fawn said. "He carried on for 20 minutes at the clinic."

"Oh, and you were going for a bravery medal yourself?" Will said. He could feel his mouth smirking. "You musta asked me 10 times how much it was gonna hurt—and don't think I didn't see you makin' a meal outa your fingernails in the waiting room."

"Was not," Fawn said. She drew her small brown hands into fists. "Take that back, Will, or I'll let you have it."

"No one's going to let anyone else 'have' anything," said a calm, dry voice from the other end of the table. "Not unless it's some more of that goat cheese. Pass me a hunk, would you, Bud? I haven't had this much protein since they started the rations. With two and a half pounds of meat a week for a whole family, I'm surprised we don't all suffer from malnutrition."

The voice was Will's mom's—Ingrid Hutchinson. As she almost always did, she was taking everything in calmly, her mouth twitching at the corners the way it did when she was amused. She rarely broke into a real smile, but that didn't mean she didn't see something funny in just about everything. Right now she wrinkled her nose with its faded freckles and nodded her head at the kids, bobbing a few dark-blonde tendrils that had popped out of the bunched-up braid at the base of her neck.

"You aren't the only ones going back to the grind," Mom said. "I have to start teaching again. Reverend Bud's taking over for Reverend Weston while he's away."

"With us having more expenses now—you know, another mouth to feed—I'm having to look for a job myself," Tina, Reverend Bud's wife, put in, "even though I'd much rather just take care of Abe and Bud."

"But you don't hear us whining, do you?" Mom said.

"You're grown-ups," Fawn said. "You aren't allowed to whine."

"Neither are you," Mom said, "because in case you two hadn't noticed, we are surrounded by everything you need to have a good time before you do have to go back to school."

Will looked out from the sunny patio at the LaFonda Hotel's café where they were sitting and had to admit she was right. The Santa Fe Fiesta was going on right in front of them, and you couldn't beat that for fun.

Santa Fe held its fiesta every Labor Day weekend. Will knew it was supposed to be in honor of some Spanish guy named DeVargas taking Santa Fe back in something like 1683 from the Indians, after *they* had taken it back from *him*. That much Will had learned in school. The rest of it he learned about at the fiesta, which lasted two and a half days every year. There were spicy Spanish sandwiches they called bocadillos, the rice dish paella, the cornbread with its surprising green chiles hidden inside—plus the songs that danced in the air from the musicians in their mariachi vests, and the Spanish people swirling their rainbow of costumes in the streets, and the throngs of Santa Feans—Hispanic, Indian like Fawn, and Anglo like Will's family—crowding the rooftops of the adobe buildings, watching for Zozobra, the big eerie figure the Spanish built every year to carry in the parade. He would officially start the whole celebration off. *That* was, in Will's opinion, the best part, because Zozobra, who represented gloom, would be burned down to ashes—the Spanish way of chasing away sad thoughts and bringing back hope. Will didn't believe that—but it was fun to watch Old Man Gloom get the torch.

He leaned out again to see if the giant, 40-foot figure had appeared yet, but, of course, he hadn't. It wasn't even close to dark.

"Him coming?" Abe said, tugging the striped sleeve of Will's cotton shirt.

Will yanked his shirt back up over his shoulder. When Big Abe tugged, he *tugged*. Still, Will was patient as he answered. Abe didn't mean to be rough *or* a pest. The way his mother explained it, Abe just hadn't been born with "as much going for him" as Will and Fawn had. She always reminded them that Abe's special talent was for love and that just as with everybody, they should look for their common ground with him rather than for their differences from him.

"Zozobra's not comin' yet," Will said. "They don't bring him out until it's time to burn him."

Tina Kates shuddered. "I still don't understand that custom. It seems kind of violent to me. Especially with the war going on and all."

"That's just the point," Will's mom said. "They burn him because he's Old Man Gloom. The fiesta is all about getting rid of gloomy thoughts for good." The corners of her mouth twitched. "As much as I laugh at their method, I'm all for getting rid of gloomy thoughts."

Will had to agree with her there. With his father probably a prisoner of war in the Pacific somewhere, and Fawn's father serving in Europe and her mother in Arizona being treated so she wouldn't go blind, and both of Abe's original Jewish parents maybe dead or in some German camp set up by Hitler—Will took a deep breath from just thinking about all of it. Yeah, they could all use a little gloom-chasing. Mom tried to keep their spirits up all the time, but the fiesta gave them an even bigger boost.

Will glanced around at the rest of the partyers milling around the LaFonda Hotel. *You'd never know there was a war going on all over the world to look at these people,* he thought. *Except for him.* Will's eye caught a man wearing steel-framed glasses and smoking a pipe. He'd been sitting there all afternoon, just staring. Every once in a while his eyebrows moved up and down together, but everything else on him was still.

Abe nudged Will with his elbow and nodded toward the man. "Why him sad?" he said.

"I don't think he's sad," Will said. "He just looks bored to me."

"Oh," Abe said, and shrugged cheerfully. As long as nobody was sad, Will knew Abe was okay with that.

"I might get used to that Zozobra character," Tina was saying, "but I don't think I'll ever get used to this spicy food."

Will looked at her in time to see her reaching for a glass of water, eyes red and swimming.

"Not water," her husband, Bud Kates, said. "That only makes it worse! Munch on a tortilla."

With a big, fleshy hand Bud handed Tina a piece of round, very flat bread and watched her happily with his big, pale eyes. Even though Bud was the assistant pastor at their church, when Will had first met him he'd reminded Will of Elmer Fudd. But he'd gotten to be kind of a substitute father for Will, and now that he was almost Abe's adoptive father, Will liked him even more. He might *look* like a cartoon character, but he knew how to make God seem real, and that was helping Will get through this war time *almost* as much as the fiesta.

"It burn me, too!" Abe suddenly cried.

He was fanning his mouth with one hand and trying to stuff an entire tortilla into it with the other.

"You have to watch out for those diced tomatoes," Will's mom said. "They look innocent enough, but they're so hot they'll make your nose run."

"Only one thing really puts the fire out," Fawn said. Her black eyes were shining, and the mouth that took up the whole lower half of her face was grinning, earlobe to earlobe.

"Let me guess," Mom said. "A malt."

"Yep—chocolate," Fawn said.

Mom's mouth twitched again, and she dug into her purse, pulled out a palm-full of change, and handed it to Will. "Scram, all three of you. You're driving me batty anyway."

"Let me give you some for Abe, Ingrid," Bud Kates said.

But Mom stopped him before he could even get his hand into his pocket. "It's my nickel this time," she said. "You can buy the next round."

Mom always says that, Will thought. *That next round that Bud's supposed to pay for never happens.*

But Will knew why. He'd heard Mom say more than once that assistant pastors didn't make that much, which was too bad, seeing how everybody else seemed to be making bunches of money since the war started.

Will didn't know too much about that part, and right now it was all he could do to keep track of Fawn as she darted through the crowd toward Alice's Soda Shop a block away. It was impossible *not* to keep track of Abe. He followed Will like a large, faithful Saint Bernard—among the dancers, around the food vendors, beneath the arms of fathers holding up their babies to look for Zozobra. Will tried to keep his eyes on Fawn's black braids flopping against the back of her bright red dress, but it was almost impossible. Finally, he turned to Abe.

"Carry me on your back, would ya?" he said. "Otherwise, we'll lose her."

Abe happily hauled tall, lanky Will onto his back with one arm and plowed through the throng of people. From above their heads, Will zoned in on Fawn and barked out directions to Abe.

"Go left! Oops—now she's back in the middle of the street—she's making a right turn—"

At the corner of the Plaza, Will suddenly tugged at Abe's butter-blond hair, and the big boy stopped.

"What are we worried about?" Will said. "*I* got the money!"

But Abe shook his head and charged ahead. "Got to find Fawn!" he cried.

Will knew there was no point in trying to reason with Abe right now. When he didn't know where one of them was, or thought anybody was in trouble, you might as well forget trying to keep him from plunging right on.

They careened around the corner that took them away from the crowd and onto Sheridan Street where the big sign with the malt pictured on it swayed in the wind. They found Fawn staring at the front of the shop.

This time Will stared too, and he motioned for Abe to put him down. Abe himself was gaping as well, lower lip hanging.

Their attention had been grabbed by a boy and a girl who were standing in front of Alice's Soda Shop. They had the black hair of both the Indians and the Hispanics in Santa Fe, but their faces were much different. They both had a golden cast to their skin, and the eyes that stared at a sign in Alice's window were tiny and almond-shaped.

Could they be Japanese? Will thought. He wasn't sure. They didn't look much like the cartoons of Tojos he had in his room—exaggerated Japanese soldier characters with big teeth and goggles. Besides, what would Japanese kids be doing here? The "Japs," as everybody called them, were the enemy in this war. Will moved a little closer, and so did Abe.

Both the children were dressed like Fawn and Will and Abe with their cotton plaids and stripes and polka dots—except that these two children's clothes looked as if they were going to wear through any minute. They were pressed and clean, but the cloth was so thin, Will could almost see through it.

In fact, all of the wide-faced, slanted-eyed people who were slowly and quietly joining the two kids in front of the shop had the same kinds of clothes on—clean, neat, and practically transparent. And all of them seemed to be looking at the same thing—a sign in Alice's window.

"What that say?" Abe muttered to Will.

Will moved in still closer, though he didn't have any trouble seeing over the people's heads. Even the adults were shorter than he was. Always pretty awkward in his lanky 12-year-old state, Will felt like he was on stilts with these people—

And then that thought, and all others, faded from his head as he read the two words written in bold black letters on the sign. NO JAPS, it said.

Before Will could even register exactly what that meant, the door to Alice's opened and a husky Anglo boy Will had never seen before stepped out, holding a vanilla ice cream cone. His reddish-blond hair gleamed like a flashlight beam next to the small sea of black heads in front of him as he stopped and, like everyone else, stared.

"What do you want?" the boy said to the little crowd.

Abe edged closer to Will.

"A chocolate soda," the boy in the thin shirt said.

Will felt his own eyebrow arch. The kid might look a little like a Tojo, but he didn't sound like one. He talked just like any American kid Will had ever known.

"Can't you read English?" the boy with the ice cream said. "It says no Japs are served here."

"But I want some ice cream," the Tojo-boy said.

A few of the adults in the small crowd shh-ed at him, but the boy tilted his chin up at the Anglo boy.

"You want ice cream?" the Anglo boy said. "Sure, I'll give you some ice cream, Jap." And then he took a bite from his cone and spit a mouthful of vanilla straight into the other boy's face.

There wasn't even a gasp from the small knot of people. The boy with the ice cream on his face stepped toward the spitter, but the girl at his side, who was a whole head shorter, began to whimper and tugged at his arm. Still, he stood with his chin pointed toward the boy who had just spat at him, his eyes in slits of hate. Abe practically crawled into Will's pocket.

How long the two boys would have stood there threatening each other with their eyes, Will didn't get a chance to find out. Just then an olive-green truck roared around the corner and swayed to a stop in front of Alice's. A man in an army uniform hopped out of the front seat and waved a stick over the heads of the Japanese group.

"All right, come on, time's up," he said in a voice that sounded interested in nothing. "Everybody in the truck."

"All those people are gonna get in the front of that truck?" Fawn whispered to Will.

"Unh-uh," Will said, and pointed. The knot of people unwound and trailed to the *back* of the truck where the driver was taking off the slatted tailgate so they could all climb in like cattle. It was then that Will noticed that each of them was wearing what looked like large price tags, hanging from their belts.

"Who *are* they?" Fawn whispered.

This time Will only shook his head. He was watching the two kids. By now the boy with the ice cream cone had strolled off, licking, but the two Japanese children seemed rooted to the sidewalk.

"Well, come on, get a move on," the army man said to them. Will had heard friendlier voices from growling dogs.

"But I wanted to get a chocolate soda," the boy said. "That's why I came today—and I only just found the shop—"

"Too bad for you," the army man said. "You see the sign. Now come on, don't make trouble. Let's go."

The little girl tugged at the boy's arm and moved toward the truck. The army man reached out a long, wiry arm and caught her up in it, yanking her away from the boy. She let out a shrill scream as the man roughly handed her to the adults in the truck. But when the army man reached for the boy, he dodged his grasp and made for the truck on his own. The driver caught him by the waistband of his dungarees and thrust him forward.

"I was getting in!" the boy said. "You didn't have to push me!"

The man ignored him and replaced the slatted tailgate and then climbed into the front seat. As the truck's engine roared to life, two pairs of hands curled around the wooden slats, and two pairs of black, almond-shaped eyes peered between the slats. Will wasn't sure, but as the truck pulled away, he thought they were looking right at him and at Fawn and Abe.

"Where they go?" Abe cried.

Will's gaze shifted from the truck to Abe's face. It was bright red, and his eyes were bulging. He looked like a confused bull about to charge.

"I don't know, Abe," Will said, "but you can't stop 'em, okay?"

Evidently it was *not* okay, because Abe lowered his big head and lunged after the now-disappearing truck.

"No, Abe!" Fawn cried.

She latched onto one of his arms while Will caught the other, but Abe shook them both off and kept on at a plodding run down the middle of Sheridan Street. Fawn started after him, and Will knew she was ready to spring right onto his back—and then Will could catch up and grab him—

But they both froze as around the corner at Marcy Street a long purple-black car suddenly appeared. Then its tires screamed and its rear end fishtailed crazily as its driver attempted to stop. There was no stopping Abe, though. With his head still pointed toward the truck in the distance, he collided, chest first, with the side of the car and skidded across its hood to the other side.

When Will got to him, Abe was motionless on the pavement.

Chapter Two

*W*ill dropped to his knees beside the silent Abe and clutched at the front of the big boy's shirt.

"Is he dead?" he heard Fawn say behind him. "He's not dead, is he, Will?"

"Abe!" Will said.

He tried to shake Abe with both hands, and when he didn't budge, Will slapped at his cheeks, now pale as custard.

"Come on now, son, wake up." That came from a tall man with wavy gray hair who dropped to his knees across from Will on the other side of Abe. He stuffed a cigar into his mouth and took Abe's face in his hands. A diamond sparkled sharply from the ring on one of his long fingers.

Will recognized him as Mr. DeWitt, who went to their church. It was a relief to have an adult there that he knew, but still he turned to Fawn and said, "Go get Bud and Tina! And Mom, too! Quick!"

"But is he dead?" Fawn said. Will had never seen her eyes so big and round.

"No, he's not dead," Mr. DeWitt said through his cigar. "Thank the Lord—he's got a pulse. I didn't even see him until it was too late to stop."

"Go get Bud!" Will said again to Fawn.

"He sure looks dead," she said, and then took off.

Part of Will wanted to run, too. Abe did look lifeless lying there.

And then his big, pale eyes fluttered open, looking confused and scared.

"It's okay, pal," Will said. He squeezed Abe's clammy hand. "It's me, Will."

The second Abe's eyes focused on Will, he smiled, and Will sucked in air. Abe's mouth was sticky-red with blood.

"Let me have a look, sonny," Mr. DeWitt said.

Abe started to pull away, but Will squeezed harder on his hand. "He's a friend," he said. "Even if he *did* try to run ya over."

He grinned at Abe, who gave him back a bloody grin. Will glanced over his shoulder. He sure wished Bud and Mom would get there.

"You didn't knock any teeth out," Mr. DeWitt said. He rocked back onto his heels and pulled a handkerchief out of the pocket of his pinstriped suit. He was chewing at his cigar like a dog gnawing a bone. Will guessed he was a little scared himself.

"I was only kiddin' about you runnin' him over," Will said. "Y'know, tryin' to joke around with him." He nodded toward Abe, who was still grinning.

"Oh, I know," Mr. DeWitt said.

He ran his long fingers along Abe's arms and legs, watching his face. Abe just kept grinning. Finally Mr. DeWitt sat back again and removed the soggy cigar from his mouth.

"Doesn't appear that anything's broken," he said. "He's a lucky boy. What the devil was he doing running down the middle of the street? I thought something was after him."

"No, *he* was after *it*," Will said. "See, what happened was—"

Will poured out the story, relief making him talk even faster than usual. It was so good to know Abe was going to be all right, it even felt like the tale had a happy ending.

But when he reached that ending—with Abe taking off after the truck with the two unhappy Japanese children peeking between the slats at them—Mr. DeWitt began to chew more fiercely on the cigar, and a red spot appeared on each of his cheeks. His eyebrows came together in a V as he glared down at Abe.

"What the devil is the matter with you, boy?" he said. His voice was tight. "No Japanese is worth worrying about, much less almost getting yourself killed over!"

Abe's eyes shifted nervously to Will. "Why him mad?" he said.

"He's not mad at you—"

"The devil I'm not! It's preposterous to risk your life for those people!" By now the veins on Mr. DeWitt's forehead were bulging, and Will thought if he chewed any harder on that cigar he was going to bite the end right off.

"They were just kids, though," Will said. "Abe can't stand to see any kid get hurt—"

"And what about our own boys?" Mr. DeWitt said. "Boys like your father over there in the Pacific. Who do you think's responsible for him being there? It's *those* people!"

He jabbed his finger down Sheridan Street as if the entire Japanese army were assembled there. Abe stuffed his fist in his mouth, a sure sign that he was about to start wailing. Will patted his shoulder.

"It's okay, Abe," he said. "Nobody's mad at you."

"Who says I'm not mad?" Mr. DeWitt said. "Those people are not to be trusted, and as far as I'm concerned, they ought to lock them in that camp and never let 'em out!"

"What camp?" Will said.

Mr. DeWitt threw his cigar to the ground as if it were one of

the Japanese in question and pulled another one from the inside
of his pinstriped jacket. Will noticed that his white shirt was so
damp with sweat, the straps of his undershirt showed right
through it.

This guy is really worked up, he thought. *Maybe I oughta just
shut up.*

But what "camp" was he talking about? A bunch of Japanese
people were camping with the army—in New Mexico?

"What camp?" he said again.

Mr. DeWitt tossed his match aside and pumped furiously at the
new cigar before he took it out to speak. "That relocation camp,"
he said. "The one just outside of town." He motioned with his
cigar. "They're set up all over the west—Colorado, Arizona, Utah,
you name it. They had to get all of them away from the California
coast. It was a military necessity."

"But why?" Will said. "Those two kids in the truck talked like
Americans."

"They call themselves Americans because they were born on
our soil," Mr. DeWitt said. "But a Jap is a Jap—it makes no differ-
ence whether he's an American citizen or not. With all of them
banded together along the Pacific, they'd have had the country
crawling with their relatives from overseas before we knew what
was happening to us. Look at Pearl Harbor—it's a known fact the
Japs living there helped with the attack."

"I didn't know that fact," Will said. "And I know a lot about
the war."

Mr. DeWitt's eyebrows wrinkled up like two caterpillars. "You
don't know as much as you think you do. You're just a kid."

"But that boy and girl in that truck were just kids," Will said.
"What damage could they possibly do?"

"They're Japs," Mr. DeWitt said into his cigar. "They got
loyalties."

"But I don't get it. My grandparents were German—they even

spoke German—and we're fighting the Germans, too, but nobody put us in some camp. And Abe here—he hardly speaks English at all, he's so German—"

Abe gave a whimper. Mr. DeWitt's eyebrows were now practically tied in a knot. "Are you saying you *like* having Japanese running all over Santa Fe?"

"I didn't say that, but—"

"Personally, I don't blame business owners like Alice there for trying to keep them out of their establishments. The Japs are just lucky they don't have enough money to be doing any banking, or I'd have a sign up in First National's window faster than you can say Tokyo. But I'll tell you one thing—" Mr. DeWitt paused long enough to spit out a piece of the cigar he'd taken off with a tooth. "I'm going to make a protest about them bringing them into town to shop and that kind of malarkey. You just can't trust them."

"But I just don't see—"

Will didn't have a chance to finish. Suddenly Fawn's voice could be heard at the end of Sheridan Street, hollering, "He's down here! Come on—hurry!"

Tina Kates nearly knocked Will over getting to Abe, and Bud was right beside her. Mom was there, too, as out of breath and red-faced as they were. Abe beamed up at all of them as if they were there to celebrate his birthday.

"I'm sorry as I can be, Reverend Kates," Mr. DeWitt said. "I didn't even see him—he just came out of nowhere and ran right into the side of my car."

Will stared at him. His voice was so concerned and kind. He didn't even sound like the same man who a minute before had been ready to string every Japanese American up by his thumbs.

"He seems to be all right," Bud said after quickly checking Abe for injuries. "Looks like he just bit down on his tongue." He grinned down at Abe. "What have I told you about using turn signals?"

"Are you *sure* he's all right?" Tina said. She was taking off Abe's shoes.

"What's she gonna do?" Fawn whispered to Will. "Check every one of his toes?"

"Did he lose consciousness at all?" Mom said.

"You bet he did!" Fawn said. "I thought he was dead lying there."

Tina gasped, but Mom's mouth twitched. "Thank you, Fawn. I can always count on you not to hold anything back."

"Are you thinking concussion?" Bud said.

"I think he needs to be checked over," Mom said. "You don't want to fool around with a head injury."

"Then get the car," Tina said. "We have to get him to the hospital right away!"

"No hospital!" Abe cried.

He sat up with a lurch that sent both Mom and Tina sprawling. Even Mr. DeWitt and Bud had trouble keeping their balance, and Abe did manage to clobber Mr. DeWitt in the shin as he fought to stand.

"Whoa, buddy," Bud said. "Take it easy now."

"No hospital!" Abe looked at Tina, his fist poised to go straight to his mouth. "You say no more doctor, Mutti! You say no shots!"

Will was sure that if Abe did get to his feet, he was going to take off running, and not even a Buick would be able to stop him this time.

Only because Bud and Mr. DeWitt were sitting on him was Abe still on the ground. He had his fist firmly crammed into his mouth, muffling the moaning that was coming straight from his terrified heart. Will squeezed in between Bud and Tina and got close to Abe's face.

"There's nothin' to be scared of, Abe," he said. "It's not like gettin' those shots. The doctors are just gonna look at your head." Will gave him a light punch on the arm. "I'm sure there's nothin' wrong with it. That head's too hard to get broken."

Abe stopped moaning, but the fist stayed where it was, and the pale eyes that looked at Will were still suspicious.

"Keep it up, Will," Bud whispered. "I think you're making progress."

"Tell you what, Abe," Will said. "What do you say I go with you and let them do everything to me that they do to you? We'll do it together."

Abe shook his head, hand still lodged in his mouth.

Think of something, Will said to himself. A bribe—that's what he always used when he wanted Fawn to do something. What did Abe like more than anything?

He had it.

"Okay, Abe," Will said, nose just an inch from Abe's. "Here's the deal: You let me go to the hospital with you, and I'll take you into the War Room tonight and tell you everything as many times as you want to hear it."

Breaths were held as slowly the fist came out.

"Promise?" Abe said.

"Cross my heart and hope to spit," Will said.

The big head finally nodded, and Bud grinned. "I knew if anybody could do it, you could, Will. He thinks you walk on water."

"Yeah, well, before Will's head swells up any bigger," Mom said, "why don't I go get your car?"

"There's no need," Mr. DeWitt said. "We can take him in mine. There's room for everybody."

"You think it still runs after that collision?" Bud said.

Tina didn't seem to think that was funny. She glared at Bud and fussed over Abe as they somehow hoisted him into Mr. DeWitt's Buick.

And as it turned out, there was no need to be worried. The doctor at St. Vincent's practically went over Abe with a microscope—with Tina supervising—and said he just had a few bumps and bruises, but that since he'd blacked out for a minute, they'd need to keep an eye on him at home for the next 24 hours.

"I think you'll be able to handle it just fine," the doctor said to Tina. "Do you have training as a nurse's aide?"

"I do," Tina said, "although I haven't done it since we moved here—"

"Abey not go home!" Abe said suddenly. "War Room."

"What's he talking about?" the doctor said.

"You don't know about the War Room?" Bud said, eyes twinkling. "There's no place you can find out more of the skinny on the war than the War Room."

Bud, of course, was talking about Will's bedroom. Abe didn't even want to stop for a malt or stay to watch Zozobra burn. He wanted to go straight to Will's and hear about everything—for about the fiftieth time, according to Will's last count.

As soon as they pulled up to the Hutchinsons' house on Canyon Road, the three kids tore up the stairs. Mom, Bud, and Tina headed for the kitchen for some of Mom's leftover strudel. Will figured Mom knew she'd better keep them occupied or Tina would be up in Will's room every seven seconds making sure Abe hadn't lapsed into a coma.

As they went up the steps, he heard the radio go on in the kitchen, playing the last few bars of a Benny Goodman tune before the news report came on. Will stopped on the steps to listen, just in case there was news on any of the battles. You could never have too many war facts, in his opinion.

But it was about money this time.

"Americans are earning more than ever before," the announcer said. "It's a pretty good war if you don't get shot at."

Will scowled and went on up to his room.

"Why you mad?" Abe said to him from the floor where he was already pulling the scrapbook out from under the bed—the one filled with clippings from *LIFE* magazine and *TIME* magazine and the Scripps-Howard newspaper.

"Because some people don't take the war seriously," Will said. "But I'm not mad at you, Abe. It's not your fault."

Abe smiled happily and patted the scrapbook. "You tell," he said.

"Don't you ever get tired of hearing about it?" Fawn said.

She evidently did, because she was lying on her back on the bed, poking with her toes at the model airplanes Will had hanging from the ceiling.

"If you break any of those, your name is Mud," Will said. He went over to the big map on the wall with the tiny magnetic planes that marked the battles and cleared his throat. "We have to start with some background, Abe."

Abe sat up, cross-legged, back straight, on the floor in front of Will and watched with his lower lip hanging down as Will went over what had happened so far in the war—mostly the part his dad was involved in.

He told Abe how three years ago, in 1941 when the U.S. had first gotten into the war, and even into 1942, the Japanese were winning all the battles in the Pacific Ocean, and it was in one of them, on the Bataan Peninsula, that Will's father, Rudy, had most likely been captured and put in a Japanese prisoner-of-war camp.

It was hard for Will to believe that his father wasn't still out there fighting, especially in 1943 when the American soldiers and their Allies had fought their way up the necklace of South Pacific islands Will pointed out to Abe on the map. They'd captured enough islands, Will explained, that American planes were able to refuel on them and go on to win the battles of the Philippine Sea, Tinian, and Guam.

The Allies—including the U.S. and England and France—now had all the Solomon Islands and could look ahead to attacking the Japanese mainland, especially since the United States had enough people and materials to keep building new ships and planes and other military stuff, and Japan didn't.

"What about where *my* dad is?" Fawn said. She was on her stomach on the bed now, chin in her hands.

"He's in the European Theatre," Will said importantly.

"Why do they call it a theatre?" Fawn said. "It's not like they're putting on a play—this is real stuff!"

"I don't know," Will said. "They just do. It's the place where stuff is happening—just like where my dad is is called the Pacific Theatre."

"So go on," Fawn said.

Will rolled his eyes at Abe and turned back to the map. "Over here in France, the D-Day operation was successful—"

"My dad was in that," Fawn said.

"We *know*. And now that General Eisenhower is Supreme Allied Commander, the Allies are driving across France to the German border, and they have the Germans on the run."

Will stopped and looked at Abe. "The bad Germans—not the good ones."

When Abe grinned, Will went on. "The Soviets—that's our allies from up here in Russia—are also chasing them. It woulda been nice, though, if those people that tried to assassinate Hitler over the summer had been successful. You remember, he's the baddest German of them all—"

Fawn hissed in agreement.

"—but a lot of people still think the war might be over by Christmas," Will said.

Abe gazed in awe at the map. Fawn came up to a sitting position on the bed.

"Do you figure you know more about the war than just about anybody, Will?" she said.

"No, silly," he said, though he did feel his chest expanding as he climbed up onto the bed to sit next to her. "I get all my facts from people that do know everything—guys like Ernie Pyle. He's that Scripps-Howard reporter that got right in the trenches with the soldiers. There's a lot of stuff we still don't know, though, because the government figures if they tell it to us, the enemy can get ahold of it, too."

"Oh, yeah," Fawn said. "I've seen those signs—'Loose Lips Sink Ships.' "

They sat in silence for a minute. Then from the floor, Abe started to snore.

"Is he un—whatever that thing was they said he was?" Fawn said, eyes popping.

"No, he's not unconscious," Will said. "He's just asleep. He always goes to sleep when I tell him about the war."

"Some bedtime story," Fawn said. "I'm gonna go down and see if there's any strudel left. You coming?"

Will shook his head, and as Fawn closed the door behind her he stretched out on his bed, hands behind his head. Above him, the model airplanes danced on their strings.

I sure wish I could just get in one of those and fly right over to the Pacific and find Dad, he thought.

No, I wish there had never been a war in the first place and Dad never had to go.

I wish—

But he stopped there. Mom always said wishing didn't make it so, but praying might. Will closed his eyes and switched his thoughts to God.

God, could You just stop this whole thing, please? Could You make the Japanese stop attacking our guys? Could You make them let Dad go? Or could You at least make sure they don't hurt him while he's there?

Will sighed. Talking about the war didn't make *him* sleepy. It always made him wide awake, thinking and worrying about his father. And *that* got him hoping terrible things would happen to the Japanese—

I sound like Mr. DeWitt, God. He sure hates the Japanese— even the ones that were born here. Is that okay with You?

God didn't answer, but Will was used to that. Since he'd really started talking to God, he'd figured out that sometimes it took a while to get a reply. You had to watch for it everywhere, too.

Will opened his eyes and looked at the map again. Was the answer up there? Were the Japanese who wanted ice cream the same ones who wanted his father as their prisoner?

If they were, he decided, Mr. DeWitt was right. He was going to have to hate them, too.

Chapter Three

*T*he fiesta was over all too soon as far as Will was concerned, and Tuesday, the first day of school, came even faster. It would have been bad enough if he'd been going back to Carlos Gilbert Elementary. At least there he knew what was what. But he didn't know what to expect at Harrington Junior High, and that was never a position he liked to be in.

It also would have been better—in his opinion—if Fawn and Abe were going with him. But Fawn was going to St. Catherine's Girls' School for sixth grade, and Abe went to the Opportunity School that was run by the nuns, down behind St. Francis Cathedral. It was a special school for kids like Abe who, as Mom always put it, weren't smart in the same way that kids in other schools were smart.

Everything is different this year, Will thought as he poked at his fried egg at the breakfast table. *I even have to ride the stupid bus instead of riding with Mom. Why did Mom have to have that accident and wreck the car?*

"Something wrong with your egg, Will?" Mom said. She was

already stuffing papers into her briefcase.

"Yeah. I'm eating it too early."

"I knew I shouldn't have let you kids sleep in so much over the summer. You've turned into slugs, both of you."

Her mouth twitched with the beginnings of a smile. Will didn't twitch his back.

"I don't mean too early in the morning; I mean too early in the year. We shouldn't be going back to school already. Look out there—it's still summer."

"September is definitely the most difficult month here," Mom said. "School is starting, but it's still warm—none of the leaves have turned. I miss Chicago this time of year." She finished buckling the briefcase and nudged Will with it. "Buck up, pal—October's on its way. And you'd better be on yours. The bus comes in five minutes. You miss it—you walk."

"You know what?" he said. "I read a lot this summer. I bet I'm way ahead of everybody else. What's the point in my even going this week? Why don't I wait and start next Monday?"

"Let's go. I want you on your way to the bus stop before Bud picks me up."

Fawn appeared just then, dressed in her crisp navy-blue-and-white St. Catherine's uniform. She wore it as if it were lined with sandpaper.

"Why's Reverend Bud picking you up?" Fawn said to Mom.

"Because we don't have a car anymore, bird brain," Will said.

"There will none of that here," Mom said. She gave Will a hard look.

"How come you're in a bad mood, Will?" Fawn said. "I'm the one who should be in a bad mood. I hate this uniform, Mama Hutchie."

"Uh-huh," Mom said. "Come on. I'll walk you to the corner." She put out her pinkie finger to Will. He took it with his, and they shook. It was their substitute for a kiss. "Try to have a good day," she said. "It doesn't take as much effort as trying to have a bad one—which you're working at pretty hard."

Will thought about that all the way to the bus stop on the corner of Canyon Road and Paseo de Peralta, all the way to the school in the back of the bus, and even as he was dawdling up the front walk toward the building, whose front doors hung open like jaws.

That's all easy for her to say. She's always telling me, "Look for the common ground." But I wasn't so pretty good at that last year. I didn't make any friends at school then; why should it be any different now?

He looked up to where a headdress of white clouds floated in a crystal-blue sky. Try to have a good day, Mom had said. *The only way I'd have a good day is if I could just fly away up there.*

But he'd learned a lot of things over the last few months, and one of them was that it paid off to listen to what Mom said. If she said try, he'd better try or it was all going to come back to haunt him. He scowled as he walked through the jaw-doors and into a wide, shiny-floored hallway whose ceiling made him feel the size of an ant.

Try to have a good day. Think about something good. Well, let's see—the Three Amigos won't be here.

Yeah, they'd still be in the boys' home after all the stealing they'd done last summer.

But somehow not having them around to torment him didn't erase the aloneness he felt as he trailed down that endless hallway to Room 12—the homeroom he'd been assigned to. Everyone else in the hall had somebody to walk with—to whisper to and then howl with—even to hit playfully with each other's lunch pails. Will gripped his with a sweaty hand and watched the brown faces of the Indians and the Hispanics who swarmed around him.

It would help if I wasn't the only Anglo in the entire place, he thought miserably.

So much for trying to have a good day.

His first three classes dragged by like the last few days before Christmas. In language arts they started right in on the parts of speech. When Will raised his hand and asked Mrs. Torres what the point was in learning about adverbs and prepositions when there was a war on, she just said, "Give us the answer to number three, please."

In math, old Mr. Marin croaked on about graphs and didn't even hear Will when he asked if they were going to be graphing the number of Japanese Tojos killed versus the number of Allied soldiers who had died.

In science, a huge woman whose last name Will couldn't even pronounce barked at them to read the first chapter in the textbook and be ready for a quiz tomorrow. Will didn't ask her anything.

But lunchtime was the period Will dreaded the most. Everybody else would crowd into the cafeteria and sit with friends and trade tortillas and tamales, while he found a corner to eat in alone. He couldn't bring himself to do it, so when the lunch bell rang, he slipped out the side door and sat down on a set of steps with his lunch pail. At least there, nobody would be staring and, worse, whispering and pointing.

Still, the cheese and tomato sandwich he chewed on turned to cardboard in his dry, unhappy mouth. He tried to focus on something else.

Sure wish there was some meat on this sandwich, he thought. *But we all hafta help with the war effort. They're rationing meat so the boys on the front can have some.*

He wondered if the Japanese were giving his dad any.

"Excuse me," said a voice behind him. "Is this where you're supposed to be, son?"

Will jerked around so fast he dropped his sandwich on the steps. He leaned down to get it and looked up at the same time. The face that looked down at him was weathered-looking—and stern. The man's eyes squinted as if he were looking into the sun. Will concluded right away that this wasn't a face he ought to argue with.

"No, sir!" Will said. He jammed the sandwich into his pocket and scrambled up. The more he stood up, the taller the man seemed. His belt with its big turquoise buckle was high, and slender legs extended endlessly down to a pair of high-heeled leather cowboy boots.

"Where *are* you supposed to be?" the man said in a voice that, surprisingly, didn't *sound* like he was herding cattle. From the white combed-back hair and string tie to the pointy-toed boots, he looked like he *ought* to be, though.

"Not here!" Will said—and just in case the man *did* have a cattle prod on him, he snatched up his lunch pail and hightailed it inside the building where he took off in the direction of his fourth-period class.

"No running in the halls!" the hall monitor shrilled at him.

You don't understand! Will wanted to shout at her as he slowed to a double-time walk. *I* have *to run! Getting in trouble the first day isn't going to sound like a "good day" to my mom!*

For once he was glad to hear a bell signaling the start of the next class, and he escaped into the social studies room still looking over his shoulder for the stern white-haired man who looked like he could rope a calf with one hand. At the front of the room a square-looking woman with black hair down to her waist was writing on the board: *Mrs. Rodriguez.*

Why don't I have even one teacher with a name like Smith or Jones? Will thought. And then he slipped into a desk and waited for another boring assignment.

But when the bell rang, Mrs. Rodriguez didn't call out page numbers. She leaned against her desk and surveyed the class with bright, black eyes. They were the only things on her that didn't look square, Will thought.

"This is a social studies class, people," she said.

At least she isn't calling us "boys and girls," Will thought.

"That means we'll be studying what's going on in the world. And what is the biggest thing on everyone's minds right now?"

"Recess," a voice behind Will whispered.

Will turned around, and he could feel his eyes popping. It was a white kid, an Anglo. Will was sure he'd never seen him before—and yet, somehow he looked familiar.

"How about you?" Mrs. Rodriguez said. "What's on your mind?"

Will slowly turned around. Her bright, black eyes were looking right into him.

"Is it something that's behind you?" she said.

"No," Will said quickly. "The war's what's on most people's minds."

"Correct," Mrs. Rodriguez said through her square mouth. "So it seems to me that we ought to focus our study on that as much as we can. Now, the United States has been in the fighting for three bitter years."

Will's hand shot up. She nodded at him.

"It's actually only been 33 months," Will said.

Mrs. Rodriguez stared at him for a moment and then said, "All right. Thirty-three months. In that time, the tide of the war has turned. From a losing start—"

Will's hand went up again, almost of its own doing.

"Yes?" the teacher said. Her voice now had an edge to it.

"It's not good to say it was a 'losing' start," Will said. "That makes it sound like we didn't know what we were doing. The fact is, we just had to get all our fighting resources mobilized."

"Are you speaking English?" the kid behind him whispered. Will didn't dare turn around this time, nor did he want to. Mrs. Rodriguez was beginning to irritate him a little. If she was going to teach about the war, at least she could get it right. The resentment he'd been feeling all day was gathering like a storm in his chest.

Mrs. Rodriguez gave him another long look and then turned and pulled down a map that was rolled up at the top of the chalkboard. She picked up a pointer. "Once we 'got our fighting resources mobilized,' " she said stiffly, "we were able to take these islands—" She poked at the map with the long pointer. "Guadalcanal. The Solomon Islands. The Gilbert Islands. The Mariana Islands. That includes Guam and New Britain. Now we still have to take—"

Once more, Will couldn't keep his hand from going up. Mrs. Rodriguez tapped the pointer into her other palm and nodded at him. The class stirred restlessly.

"You tell her," the boy behind him whispered.

"You forgot Bismarck Archipelago," Will said.

A half-Anglo boy with glasses two seats over said, "Wow." Several of the girls giggled and tried to say it. Mrs. Rodriguez cut them all short with a look.

"That was a relatively minor battle in the grand scheme of things," she said.

This time, Will didn't even bother to raise his hand. It was as if the whole rotten day was stirring together with the mess this woman was making of the Allied victories. His mouth just opened and started frothing forth words all by itself.

"I bet you wouldn't say that to the men who fought in that battle!" he said. "Or to the kids of the guys that died."

"You are out of line, young man—"

"If they hadn't of won that battle, how do you think we could go on and take the Philippines or the rest of the islands?"

"That's enough—"

"You shouldn't be standing up there making *any* battle look little! If you can't teach about the war right, you shouldn't oughta be teachin' about it at all!"

"That is quite enough!"

Will stopped because he had run out of breath. Only then did he realize that Mrs. Rodriguez's nostrils were flaring, and the bright, black eyes were flashing.

"You are excused," she said. "Go down to Mr. Tarantino's office—and take this."

She turned sharply to her desk, her long hair flapping out behind her, and scrawled something on a piece of paper. The storm in Will's chest was now a giant ball of fear.

"Who's Mr. Tarantino?" he muttered.

"I think that's the principal," the kid behind him muttered back.

His thought was right. The sign on the office door the hall monitor directed Will to said: MICHAEL TARANTINO, PRINCIPAL. But that wasn't the worst of it.

The man who opened the door to him was the tall, white-haired, tanned-faced man who'd found him on the steps—the one who looked as if he could rustle cattle with his bare hands.

Chapter Four

*O*h," was all Will could say as he watched the tall man hook his thumbs into his belt. He wanted to look around for a cattle prod, but he didn't dare move his eyes from Mr. Tarantino's squinting gaze.

"We meet again," the principal said. "Looks like this isn't your day."

"No, sir," Will said. He wanted to add: *You have no idea.*

Mr. Tarantino held out his hand, and Will put Mrs. Rodriguez's note in it. He would rather have cut off a finger and given *it* to him.

"Have a seat," Mr. Tarantino said, and he nodded to a chair that Will saw was made out of a saddle. The principal sat in an identical one that faced it. Will wished he could ride away on it— far, far from here.

He waited, heart pounding in his ears, while Mr. Tarantino read the note. *Here it comes,* Will thought. *He's going to lower the boom. I'm as good as dead. And Mom's sure to finish the job when I get home.*

"Will Hutchinson," Mr. Tarantino said. He folded the note and tossed it onto the corner of his desk.

"Yes, sir."

"Are you any relation to Ingrid Hutchinson over at Carlos Gilbert?"

It was all Will could do not to fall to his knees and beg the man to put him out of his misery right there. He *knew* Mom? This couldn't get any worse.

"Yes, sir," Will said. "She's my mother."

"You're blessed, then. Fine woman, your mother." Mr. Tarantino leaned back and folded his hands on the front of his Western-style shirt. "What's she going to say when you have to tell her you were sent to the principal's office the first day of school?"

Will couldn't answer. He could only draw his finger across his throat. Mr. Tarantino nodded solemnly.

"Sounds about right. She's a tough lady."

"You don't know the half of it," Will said.

"Of course, she would have to be—what with your father a war prisoner and her trying to look after you and the little Indian girl. I have to admire her."

"Me, too," Will said miserably.

Mr. Tarantino nodded again and fiddled for a moment with the ends of his string tie. Then he glanced at his wristwatch with the turquoise stones on the band.

"You were only in Mrs. Rodriguez's class for 10 minutes. Didn't take you long to get yourself in hot water. Am I right to assume you walked in there with a chip already on your shoulder?"

"You mean, was I already messed up inside?"

"Something like that."

"Yes, sir," Will said. He took a hard swallow. It didn't look like

Mr. Tarantino was going to break out a paddle or anything, but this was still pretty scary.

"Does it have anything to do with the fact that you were eating outside alone instead of joining the other students in the cafeteria?" the principal said.

Will hesitated. If he admitted that, he'd probably start whining and maybe even start bawling. He'd rather be paddled to within an inch of his life.

"I'm going to take that as a yes," Mr. Tarantino said. "I know how hard it is to be an Anglo in this neck of the woods. You and I share that problem."

Will felt his eyebrows go up in surprise.

"The tan helps me look a little more like the natives," Mr. Tarantino went on. "And the white hair makes my skin look even darker. But in the final analysis, I'm an Anglo, and that means I've had to work pretty hard to be accepted. Are you having that same experience?"

"Yeah!" Will said. "I never went to school before last year 'cause my mom always tutored me 'til she went to work. I tried to make friends—I really did—but I kind of messed up with some of the Hispanic kids and now I guess the word's gotten around that I'm trouble. But I'm not! You can ask Fawn—that Indian girl my mom took in—and Abe—he's Reverend Kates's adopted kid—you know, from over at the Presbyterian church—they're my best friends, only they don't go here—and you can only stand bein' by yourself when everybody else's got people to hang around with for so long before you get mad—and then Mrs. Rodriguez, she started saying stuff about the war that isn't true—and I guess I just had enough—only, I shouldn'ta said the stuff I did. My mom's gonna put me on restriction for the rest of my life. Can't you just give me swats and not tell her about this?"

Will stopped to breathe. He hadn't meant to blurt out all of that, but Mr. Tarantino just kept watching him and nodding as he talked, and even while he was squinting, he didn't look like he thought Will was a stupid little kid.

"I don't believe in swats in this office," Mr. Tarantino said finally. "That only makes boys your age resentful as far as I can see, and I certainly don't need a mob of adolescents plotting revenge against me." He rubbed a finger along his weathered cheek. "But I do believe in consequences for poor judgment—and your conduct with Mrs. Rodriguez was poor judgment, don't you agree?"

"It was the worst judgment I probably ever made," Will said.

"You have a strong sense of the dramatic, Will. Now—I like for the consequences I give not only to punish, but to help the perpetrator learn."

"What's a perpetrator?" Will said.

"That's you, in this case. The one who does the dirty deed."

"Oh."

"I think the appropriate consequences in this case should be as follows—"

Will sucked in a sharp breath. This was going to involve some long letter of apology to Mrs. Rodriguez that Mom was going to have to sign, too. He could just feel it coming on.

"—every day during lunchtime, you are to come here to my office and I'll put you to work. You'll have time to eat your lunch, of course, and then I'll make you my office boy. Is that clear?"

Will was afraid to answer, for fear Mr. Tarantino would think he was too overjoyed and think of something really horrible. He just pumped his head up and down.

"Any questions?" Mr. Tarantino said.

"Just one," Will said carefully. "What about my mom?"

"What about her?"

"Are you going to call her or something?"

"Do I need to?"

"No!" Will said. He could only contain himself for so long.

"Let's do this. Let's see if your classroom behavior improves as you spend more time with me. If it doesn't, then we'll bring your mother into it. I think she has enough on her mind right now without worrying about your school conduct, don't you?"

"I couldn't agree with you more, Mr. Tarantino," Will said in the most adult voice he could manage.

"Most of the students just call me Mr. T. It saves time."

"Sure, Mr. T.," Will said. "Can I go now?"

"There's just one more thing." Mr. T. stopped fiddling with his tie and leaned forward, his elbows on his knees. He stretched out his hands in front of him as he went on. "Around here, our vocabulary doesn't include the word failure. If we let you kids fail, our future civilization is in trouble." The index fingers of both hands pointed at Will. "I'm not going to allow you to fail. You will succeed here in every way possible. I'll see to it."

Will tried to swallow again, but this time he couldn't. For some reason he couldn't figure out, he felt like he might cry.

Now *I start bawling!* he thought as he scrambled to get out of the office with Mr. T.'s pass back to class in his hand. *What's the matter with me?*

There had just been something about the way Mr. T. had talked to him, never raising his voice, even being a little bit funny and a lot nice. And his hands had moved just like—

Just like Will's dad's.

Will suddenly missed his dad's hands—the way they looked when he painted—the way one of them would rest on Will's shoulder sometimes when they talked—the way he and Mom and Will always held hands at the table when they were praying.

He had to blink tears away before he could go back to class and apologize to Mrs. Rodriguez. But he couldn't get the thought of his dad out of his mind the rest of the day, and he was lost in it on the way home on the bus that afternoon as he stared out the window.

Dad had never lived in Santa Fe with them—he'd joined the

army before Will and his mother had moved away from the Los Alamos Boys' School back in 1941. But still, he seemed to be everywhere Will looked.

The warm mud-colors of the round-cornered adobe buildings reminded Will of the shades in Dad's paintings. The red and blue and yellow ceramic tiles that decorated everything made Will think of the funny stuff Dad said that popped up at all the right times to make things brighter. The thick adobe walls with their wrought-iron gates brought back memories of Dad lifting Will up so he could walk on one at Los Alamos, clinging to his hand—his long-fingered, wonderful hand—

Stop it! Will scolded himself. *He's not here, so stop it!*

He tried to keep his mind on the buildings they were passing. There was the First National Bank of Santa Fe. Will looked to see if Mr. DeWitt had gotten a "No Japs" sign up in the window yet. There was the public clock that looked like a giant pocket watch, hanging outside the jewelry store. It seemed to move as slowly as the people in the sleepy, pokey Plaza in the center of town. There were few shoppers on the three sides of the Plaza that housed the curio shops and the Woolworth's and the office buildings, and even the front of the long, porchlike Governor's Palace didn't have as many Indians selling their wares as usual. *Yeah,* Will thought, *summer is definitely over.*

There *was* one man standing in front of the Palace who caught Will's eye, and he leaned closer to the bus window to get a better look. It sure looked like the guy he and Abe had spotted at La-Fonda on Friday—the one who looked like he wasn't having such a good time. He didn't look exactly overjoyed today, either. He was leaning against one of the slim lodgepole posts on the Palace porch listlessly smoking a pipe and looking over the tops of his steel-rimmed spectacles at nothing, as far as Will could tell.

He wanted to figure out what the man was so interested in— since there was nothing better to do to try to keep his mind occupied. But the bus turned down a side street and pulled up in front of the Maytag store to let out some kids who lived nearby. The owner sold washing machines on one side of the store and music on the other. Will looked to see if he had a "No Japs" sign, but the only thing taped on his window was the Hit Parade list.

Some kids jumped off the bus, and the driver had just closed the door and started to cruise on down the street when he suddenly slammed on the brakes. The bus skidded sideways, and Will's face slid forward along the window glass. Even though he grabbed onto the seat in front of him, Will tumbled out into the aisle. Every girl on the bus seemed to squeal, and a bunch of the boys hollered things like "Hey!" and "What's goin' on?" But above it all, Will could clearly hear the bus driver yelling.

"Get out of the road, ya stupid Jap! What are ya doin' around here anyway?"

There was a short silence on the bus as the kids all scrambled back to their windows, Will included. It was hard to see over all the bobbing heads, but Will did get a glimpse of a tall, dark-haired teenaged boy wearing a knit cap loping across the road in front of the bus, a book in his hand. Even as Will was craning to see, the boy turned to look at the driver. He was Japanese—and he looked surprised.

"Go on—get out of the road!" the bus driver yelled again.

This time, the kids on the bus joined him. Windows opened, and brown heads poked their way out to shout:

"Go back to your camp, yellow vermin!"

"We don't want you here, ya Nip!"

"You're a lousy traitor!"

Will poked his head out, too, but he didn't say anything. He only watched as the Japanese boy hurriedly stuffed the book he was carrying into his back pocket and broke into a jog toward a work truck parked on the other side of the road, where in the back a whole gang of Japanese boys waved and called to him. Will couldn't hear what they were saying over the shouting from the bus.

They're probably telling him he was an idiot for reading while he was walking across the street, Will thought.

Around him, a chant was starting. "All Japs go away! No Japs in Santa Fe!"

The Japanese boy had to have heard the whole busload of kids chanting at him at the tops of their lungs, but he didn't turn his head again as he swung himself up into the back of the truck. Will had to admire him for that. It had to be hard not to shout back.

"Hey," said a voice behind Will. "What's the matter with you?"

"Huh?" Will said.

He turned around to see the Anglo boy, the one who sat behind him in Mrs. Rodriguez's class. He was standing up, so that for the first time Will saw that he was a big, husky kid. Right now, his very blue eyes were gleaming out from his very freckled face. He shoved his hand back through his curly, strawberry-blond hair.

"I said, what's the matter with you?" the boy said. "You a Jap-lover or something?"

Suddenly it came to Will where he'd seen this kid before social studies class. He was the kid who had spit at the Japanese boy in front of Alice's Soda Shop.

"No, I'm not a Jap-lover!" Will said.

"Then why aren't you yellin'?"

Freckle Boy jerked his head toward the side of the bus where all the kids were practically purple-faced from chanting, "All Japs go away! No Japs in Santa Fe!"

"If you aren't a Jap-lover, you gotta yell!" Freckle Boy said. "That's a rule!"

It was a rule Will hadn't heard of, but at the moment it made an odd kind of sense. He *was* the only person on the bus not chanting, including the bus driver.

Will could feel the freckled boy's blue eyes on him as slowly

Will leaned out his window again and said, "All Japs go away!" He wasn't as loud as the other kids—at least, not until Freckle Boy joined him in the window and chimed in. That made it easier to keep yelling, over and over, until the truck full of Japanese young men pulled away. It did strike Will that not a single one of them yelled anything back.

The truck had disappeared around the corner and the bus had started to move on before heads were pulled back in and the chanting faded. When Will sat down in his seat again, the freckled boy sat with him.

"I'm Herb Vickers," he said.

"Hi," Will said. "I'm Will. Will Hutchinson."

"Nice to meet ya." He lowered his voice a notch. "I'm sure glad there's another Anglo on the bus. I hate feelin' like the Lone Ranger or somethin'."

"Yeah," Will said.

"So—maybe we could pal around together."

Will knew his eyes looked surprised, but it was hard not to be. He'd never had somebody just ask to be his friend before. He nodded, of course. It was just about the first good thing that had happened to him all day.

"We got a lot in common, you and me," Herb said. His voice was as husky as he was, although every now and then he squeaked a word, as if he were for an instant going back to the way he'd talked when he was a little kid. It was funny-sounding, but Will had a feeling you didn't laugh at Herb Vickers.

"We're both about the only full Anglos in the whole seventh grade," he was saying. "And we both hate the Japs—right?"

"Oh, yeah, right," Will said. "They've got my dad!"

"My cousin's fightin' 'em. Hey—you got a bike?"

"Yeah!"

"Then we're set."

Herb stuck out a hamlike hand, and Will put his in it. What they were shaking on, Will wasn't sure. But it sure felt good to have somebody to talk to.

Chapter Five

*B*eing able to say he'd met a friend made it easier at the dinner table that night for Will to steer clear of any mention of his visit to Mr. T.'s office.

"We're gonna hang around together and ride bikes after school," Will told his mom as she dished out the macaroni and cheese.

"But not tomorrow," she said. "Bud wants to talk to you after school."

"About what?"

"Do I look like Bud to you?" Mom said. "He'll tell you when he sees you. He's taking you to Woolworth's. He says the sodas are on him."

"What about me?" Fawn said.

"He just asked for Will. And don't start balling up your fists—I think he just has something he wants Will to do for him."

Fawn smiled smugly at Will. "I bet you have to dust hymnbooks with him or something."

"You've got to be kidding," Mom said. "That doesn't sound like Bud's kind of fun. I'm sure he'd rather eat that kale you're pushing around on your plate than have a kid dust anything."

"I don't like kale," Fawn said through her teeth.

"Put some vinegar on it."

"Yeah, Reverend Bud's pretty swell," Will said. "You think he'd mind if I brought Herb with me?"

"Mind? I think he'd kiss your feet if you introduced him to another kid."

"Yuck," Fawn said.

Mom's mouth twitched as she pushed the vinegar cruet toward Fawn. "Do you have a stone in your shoe, Fawn, or did you just have a bad day?"

"I hated my day!" she said. "I'm used to being with Will and Abe all the time, and now I'm stuck with a bunch of girls at school and all they talk about is their stupid hair and their stupid dolls and every other stupid thing. It's—stupid!"

"But is it stupid?" Will said.

Fawn jabbed her fork toward him.

"Big adjustment for you," Mom said. "It's pretty tough for you right now, but I've been thinking you needed some girlfriends."

"Why? They're stu—"

"They're not like you right now," Mom said. "That's what it is. Now what do I always tell you kids when people are different from you?"

Fawn stabbed stubbornly at her macaroni.

"Psst!" Will hissed at her. "Find common ground."

"Find common ground," Fawn said.

"Thank you, Will," Mom said dryly. She looked at Fawn. "Every one of those girls can't be completely different from you. Look for somebody with at least one thing you have in common."

"Like what?"

"Like, they have two legs, two eyes—"

"Will—bag it," Mom said. "You know what I mean, Fawn. Look for somebody else who feels like she doesn't fit in. That's a good start."

"I wish I could just go to school with Will."

Will opened his mouth to say he wished the same thing, but he shut it. Maybe it was better to keep the focus off of himself on this subject.

"In the first place, you aren't old enough yet," Mom said patiently. "And in the second place, Margretta is paying your tuition to go to St. Catherine's. When she comes back from Arizona with your mother, you can discuss it with her. Until then, I think you can handle it." Mom's mouth twitched again. "I've never seen anything you couldn't handle—but try not to do it with your fists, okay?"

Fawn nodded, scowling, but later that evening she did fly into Will's room, pin him to the floor, and make him promise he wouldn't like this Herb kid more than he liked her.

"Do I have a choice?" Will said. But he promised her. "He can be your friend, too," he told her. "Maybe the day after tomorrow I'll introduce you to him."

"Why not tomorrow?"

"Because tomorrow I'm taking him with me to meet Bud."

But when Will brought up the subject with Herb the next day in social studies class—*before* the bell rang—Herb looked at Will as if he had an extra nose growing out of his forehead.

"Hang around with a pastor?" he said. "No thank *you*. It's bad enough I gotta go to church *and* Sunday school every Sunday."

"What church do you go to?" Will said.

"It's down on East Palace. It's boring there."

"Ours is pretty swell," Will said.

"Nah—I'll just meet ya tomorrow. Or, hey—what about lunch?"

Will paused. He had to go to Mr. T.'s office at lunch. Would it be a good idea to tell Herb that was his punishment? Herb might think he was a slob or something.

"I got somethin' I gotta do at lunch," Will said.

Herb's blue eyes narrowed, folding up the freckles around them. "Do you wanna hang around with me or not?"

"Yeah!" Will said quickly. "Tomorrow after school. You can meet me at the Plaza and we'll ride bikes."

The eyes stayed narrowed, and then Herb stuck out his meaty hand to shake. Will was getting the idea that this is what Herb did to seal everything. He felt like he'd just signed the Constitution or something.

Bud was waiting out in front of Harrington that afternoon in the ancient Chevrolet. It was getting more dilapidated by the day, but somehow they made it to Woolworth's, stalling only once.

"I've considered giving this thing to your mother," Bud hollered over the clang of the motor. "I hate seeing a woman alone without a vehicle. But I think she's safer walking!"

When they were settled in at the counter with sodas, Will couldn't stand the suspense any longer. "So Mom says you have something you want me to do," he said.

"You like to get right to the point, don't you, pal? All right, here's the deal. Tina has gotten herself a job." His pale eyes clouded. "I hated to see her do it. She loves being at home, especially when Abe gets in from school—you know, she likes to have the cookies and the lemonade waiting for him and all that mother stuff."

"Yeah," Will said, although that had never been *his* mother's "stuff."

"Anyway, she's going to be working two days a week as a

nurse's aide at St. Vincent's. I guess that doctor was pretty impressed with her the other day when we took Abe in."

"She practically took the stethoscope right out of his hand," Will said.

Bud chuckled. "She'll be running the place before they know it. It's perfect for her, except that on those two days she won't be home when Abe comes in from school. That's a problem."

"She doesn't want Abe by himself."

"Right. He could do it, but you know how upset he gets when he's lonely."

Will resisted the urge to stick his fist in his mouth. He just nodded.

"Now, the hospital did say that Abe could come there after school for the few hours she'll have left on her shift—"

"That's even more of a problem!" Will said. "He hates hospitals. He'd sit in a corner and cry the whole time."

"Bingo. So, we were wondering if you would be willing to spend time with Abe on Tuesday and Thursday afternoons, just until Tina comes home. We wouldn't be able to pay you, but—"

"Pay me to be Abe's friend?" Will said. "Jeepers, no. I'll do it for free. I like hanging around with Abe."

For a squirmy moment, Will thought Bud was going to cry. His eyes misted over, and he pinched the bridge of his pudgy nose. Will slurped loudly on his soda straw.

"You don't know how much we appreciate this," Bud said finally. "He trusts you like he does almost nobody else."

"When do I start?" Will said.

"Next Tuesday." Bud shook his head. "It's going to be an adjustment for all of us, especially Tina. I'm going to have to concentrate on being extra good to her, help her out more."

Will nodded, not only for Bud but for himself. It was one of those Bud-moments when he knew Bud was hinting that Will ought to do the same for his own mom. Will was always glad Bud didn't come right out and lecture him.

"Anyhow," Bud said, "we can't thank you enough."

"It's nothin'," Will said. But he could feel himself beaming.

After that, things seemed to brighten up. There was the idea of having more time to be with Abe, for one thing. And he also started to like working in Mr. T.'s office every day—even if it did mean having to make up excuses to Herb for not eating lunch with him.

One of his jobs was to announce kids that came in to see Mr. T. and usher them into his office. There was always a steady stream, mostly boys, coming in for everything from fighting on the playground to forgetting their homework for the fourth day in a row. Most of them went in looking a little green around the gills. They all came out looking relieved. Some of them were even grinning.

"There sure are a lot of kids that get into trouble," Will said to Mr. T. one day when four boys had come in during lunch hour.

"They're not all in trouble," Mr. T. said. "Some of them just need to talk." He shook his head. "Most of the ones that *have* gotten themselves into hot water are just missing their dads and they don't know how else to get that anger out of there except to act up." He squeezed Will's shoulder with a gnarly, tanned hand. "You'd know about that. How is it going in Mrs. Rodriguez's class now?"

Actually, it wasn't going badly, but it wasn't great, either. Will never took his eyes off of her during fourth period and did everything he was supposed to and even said "yes ma'am" to her. But he still didn't think she knew as much about the war as he did. She let him add facts to her lectures, but she didn't do it with a smile. Even Herb noticed it and would always whisper from behind him, "You tell 'er, Will."

One day, when he and Will were walking down the hall

together as they did all the time now, Herb said, "I know why you kiss up to Mrs. Rodriguez."

"What's that mean—kiss up to her?" Will said.

"You know—act so nice and mannerly to her when you really don't want to. It's because of your parents, right?"

"Well, sort of," Will said. "My mom says I gotta be polite."

"Yeah, mine too. Aren't parents a pain?"

Will had never thought of Mom as being a "pain," but he nodded anyway, and he wasn't sure why.

There *was* one thing Mrs. Rodriguez taught the class that Will wasn't familiar with already, and that was about unions. That, she told them, was when workers formed organizations so they could get fair pay and good working conditions. There was a union for just about every profession, Will found out—truckers, plumbers, mechanics, even actors. He liked hearing how they stood up for their rights, especially when labor leaders like John L. Lewis got them all stirred up to carry signs and hold sitdown strikes.

"I wish we could do that at school," Herb said to him that afternoon when they were riding their bikes. "If we didn't like the homework, we could just all get together and refuse to do it."

"I guess you could do it if the teachers were really loading us up and it wasn't fair," Will said.

Herb laughed. "Nah. I just want to see it outlawed altogether!"

They hung around together every day after school that week. As soon as Will got off the bus, he raced home and got on his bike and rode to the Plaza to meet Herb, who was also on his bike. From there, Herb took over. He had a different plan for them each day.

One afternoon they went chili-pepper snatching. Every fall, scarlet necklaces of chili peppers—called *ristras*—hung from porches and rooftops and balconies everywhere in Santa Fe. It was a rare household that didn't grow some, and everyone hung them up to dry for making chili powder that would make your eyes water.

Herb taught Will how to snatch a few from each *ristra* without getting caught. Will hesitated a little at first, but Herb said, "They got plenty. Don't worry about it. That stuff grows like weeds."

"So—why do we need to take it, then?" Will said.

"Because we can!" Herb said.

The second part of the game was to see who could stand to eat the most without having to grab a tortilla to stop the mouth-burning. Will won hands down; he was used to spicy food and Herb wasn't. That's when he learned that Herb was one of the summer people whose family came in June and usually left on Labor Day.

"My parents like it here better'n Ohio, I guess," he told Will. "So we're stayin' this year. At first I was mad, but now that I got somebody to pal around with, it's all right." Then, of course, he stuck his hand out for Will to shake it.

Later that day Herb decided they would hide behind the cottonwood trees in the Plaza and jump out and scare the Hispanic girls who were roller-skating on the crisscrossing sidewalks. Will commented that his foster sister would pound him if he ever did something like that to her.

"She's not one of these uppity Mexicans, though," Herb said. "They think they own the place."

"They kind of do," Will said. "I mean, it was Spanish people who founded the town."

"Yeah, but it's America now," Herb said. "And we Anglos are the true Americans."

Will would have argued—of course—except that just then the bells in St. Francis Cathedral started ringing, signaling that it was five o'clock.

"I gotta get home," Will said.

"Jeepers," Herb said. "Your mom's a lot stricter than my parents." His blue eyes took on that shine they had—which Will had decided was more of a gleam than a sparkle. " 'Course, my parents could try to be strict with me and it wouldn't do them any good."

Will didn't hang around to find out exactly what that meant. Supper would be ready at 5:15 and he had to be there to set the table.

"I'll see ya tomorrow," he said as he straddled his bike.

"Hey, I got an idea," Herb said. "How's about I come to your house tomorrow after school so when it's five o'clock you don't gotta leave? We could have more time to do stuff."

"Sure," Will said. "I live on Canyon Road."

"I've never been there," Herb said. "How do you—"

"I'll tell you tomorrow," Will said. He was already pedaling off.

"You gotta get your mom to loosen up on you," Herb called to him.

Sure, Will thought, grinning to himself. *And while I'm at it, I'll get the moon to turn purple or somethin'.*

Will got home in half the usual time and was breathing a sigh of relief when he slid in the back door at 5:05. That breath was knocked right out of him when Fawn jumped him from behind and toppled him to the kitchen floor.

"Hey!" Will cried. "What's goin' on? Let me up, Fawn!"

"Not 'til you tell me why you're ditching me every day after school!"

"What? I'm not ditching you! I'm hanging around with Herb."

"I thought you said he was gonna be my friend, too."

"He will be," Will said. "Now let me up. I gotta set the table."

"Since when were you so anxious to do that," he heard Mom

say from above him. "Don't let him up 'til you get everything you want out of him, Fawn."

"Mo-om!" Will wailed.

"When's he gonna be my friend too?" Fawn said.

"Tomorrow," Will said through clenched teeth. "He's coming over here after school."

Fawn sat back so that Will could roll out from under her and scramble to his feet. Mom twitched her mouth at him. "She's been going wild for the last half hour," she said. "You'd better let her know of your whereabouts from here on out."

"Tomorrow," Will said stubbornly to Fawn. "We'll be here when you get home."

"You better be," Fawn said.

That wasn't hard to arrange. Fawn didn't get out of school until four, and by 3:15, Herb was already at the front door. When Will got there, he was standing on the front porch, the *portale* as the Santa Feans called it, looking the place over.

"Oh," Herb said when Will opened the door. "So you do live here. Huh."

"Why?" Will said.

"Well—" Herb shrugged. "It doesn't look like the rest of the houses. It sure doesn't look like our place."

"Where's your place?" Will said.

Herb's eyes narrowed almost suspiciously. "East Palace. How come yours is different?"

It was Will's turn to shrug. "It's what they call Territorial style. Back from when New Mexico was a territory and not a state yet."

"Oh, well, that's boring stuff anyway," Herb said. "What did your father do before he went in the army?"

"He taught art."

"Oh. That explains it."

Explains what? Will wanted to say. But Herb had already

walked into the living room and was looking it over, too. It was cool and bright in there in the afternoon light. Will liked it at that time of day, especially the window seat with the pillows and the kiva fireplace and all of Dad's paintings on the wall. Herb, however, gave it a sweeping glance and said, "Where's your room?"

Will led him upstairs, already grinning. He was sure Herb was going to be impressed with his scrapbook and map and model airplanes. As usual, Herb surprised him. He took one look at the wall poster of cartooned Tojos with their big teeth and oversized goggles and said, "Swell! Do you got any darts?"

"Yeah," Will said. "What for?"

"Get 'em out. I'll show you."

Will felt a little irritation between the shoulder blades. Herb always decided what they were going to do. He'd thought since they were at his house, he'd get to do the deciding today. But since Mom had always insisted he be decent to guests, Will reached into the top of his closet and pulled down his box of darts. Herb grabbed one and let it fly at the poster, nailing a Tojo squarely between the goggled, slanted eyes.

"Take that, ya lousy Jap!" he shouted. And then he snatched up another dart.

When he'd emptied the box, he went to the poster to pull them out.

"You wanna see my scrapbook?" Will said quickly.

"I guess," Herb said.

He flopped down on Will's bed and looked down to where Will sat cross-legged on the floor.

"These clippings are from when my dad first left, back in '41," Will said. "We didn't know it then, but he got captured in this battle."

"Who's this?" Herb said. He pointed to a cartoon of Winston

Churchill, the British prime minister, puffing on a ridiculously long cigar.

"That's Churchill," Will said. "They say he smokes two-foot-long cigars. I don't believe it. Then here's the clippings from Guadalcanal, 'cause I thought my dad might be there—"

"Two feet long?" Herb said. "Can you imagine? If we got us a couple of those, we could sit in this window and smoke all night and blow the smoke out so your mom wouldn't know."

Herb moved to the window to demonstrate, but his mouth stopped before the first imaginary puff. "Hey, who's that girl?" he said, pointing outside.

Will climbed up to join him. Fawn was hurrying up the front walk, already pulling off her red neckerchief in anticipation of changing into play clothes.

"That's Fawn, my foster sister," Will said. "She's pretty swell for a girl. She can wrestle—"

"Will she be coming in here?"

"Of course," Will said. "I told her—"

"Let's hide under the bed and scare the daylights out of her!"

"I don't think that's such a good idea," Will said. "You don't know Fawn—"

But Herb was already halfway under the bed and was yanking at Will's leg.

"Come on!" he said. "I can already hear her coming up the steps!"

Will wrenched his leg away from Herb's big-ham grip, but he did join him under the bed. It looked like there was nothing to do but let Herb find out about Fawn for himself.

Fawn, as it turned out, didn't go to her room to get out of her uniform, but burst right into Will's, yelling, "Hey, Will, where's that Herb guy?"

Will could see her feet stopping short just inside the doorway, and he could feel Herb shaking with silent laughter beside him. As Fawn stepped slowly toward the bed, Herb eased his hands forward, fingers already poised as if to grab her by the ankles. Just as he took the last inch to the fringe on the bedspread, Fawn's feet suddenly disappeared. Will felt the bed bounce above them, but it was too late for Herb. He was already lunging out from under it—just in time for Fawn to jump squarely in the middle of his back.

"Hey!" Herb shouted.

Will couldn't hold back. He was snorting out guffaws before he could even crawl out from under the bed. Fawn had Herb in a stranglehold, and he was squalling like a caught piglet.

"Let me go!" Herb said, his voice slipping into one of its highs from younger days. "Let me go or I'll pound you!"

"Sure, you're gonna pound me," Fawn said. "With both hands pinned behind your back."

"Get her off of me, Will!"

Will grinned. "Go on, get off of him, Fawn. You showed him enough."

"You sure?" Fawn said, eyeing the back of Herb's head.

"Yeah. He doesn't even know what's hit him yet."

With one more tug at Herb's neck, Fawn let go and hopped lightly off of Herb's back. He fumbled to his feet, his face so red that the freckles had all but disappeared. Will was by now clutching his sides, he was laughing so hard.

"What's so funny?" Herb said.

"You!" Will said. "But don't feel bad. Everybody gets it from Fawn the first time. Nobody's sneakier than she is—and nobody's got better moves—"

"She's a girl!" Herb said.

"So?" Fawn said. She doubled her fists, but Will shook his head at her.

"Sure she is," Will said. "But I told you, she's pretty swell anyway—"

"No girl is swell," Herb said. He turned his blue-eyed glare from Fawn to Will. "If she's gotta be here—I'm not!"

"Oh, come on," Will said. "She's not that bad."

"Not that *bad?*" Fawn said.

Will warded off a punch and grinned. "You'll get used to her, Herb. She used to beat me up all the time, but now that I know some of her moves—"

"Forget it!" Herb said. He stormed toward the door. "Just forget it. I don't play with girls!"

And with that he threw open the door and launched himself out into the hallway and down the stairs.

Chapter Six

*B*oth Will and Fawn stared at the now-empty doorway until they heard the front door slam. Fawn was the first to recover.

"Who needs him anyway?" she said. "If he can't take it, who needs him?"

"I do!" Will said. "He's the only friend I got at school."

"Some friend. Besides, I don't have *any* friends at school. I tried to find somebody to climb that big cottonwood tree in the school yard with me today, and everybody started whining about how they might scuff up their shoes or tear their uniforms. I'd *like* to tear my uniform—to shreds!"

Fawn took a deep breath, and then transformed her scowl into a grin. "Wanna go see if Mama Hutchie made any more strudel?"

Will flopped down on his bed. "No."

"How come?"

"I don't *know!* Just leave me alone for one minute, would ya?"

Fawn's black eyes seemed to draw closer together. "Is it because of that Herb boy?" she said. "Because if it is, you're wasting
your time. He doesn't have any common dirt with us."

"Common *dirt?* What are you talking about?"

"That thing Mama Hutchie always says."

"Common *ground*," Will said. "And he does so."

"Like what?"

"Like— I don't wanna talk about it right now!"

"Fine," Fawn said, flouncing toward the door. "If there's any
strudel, I'm eating it all."

Will couldn't have cared less about strudel or anything else
except the fact that Herb was mad and probably wasn't going to
want to hang around with him anymore. That fact was like a cloud
hanging over his head all weekend. Even on Sunday at church,
Abe couldn't cheer him up—and then Mr. DeWitt added confusion
to the cloud and made it darker.

After the service, Will finally made Abe happy by sending him
off to bring him a cup of punch from the snack table. Will was
sitting alone on the front church steps, kicking at a loose piece of
slate, when Mr. DeWitt spotted him. He was apparently on his way
to his car, but he stopped and rested his pinstriped self against the
wall.

"How's that boy?" he said. He chuckled. "The one who ran into
my car last week."

"He's fine," Will said.

"He has a better chance of staying that way if he'll stop worrying about the Japs." Mr. DeWitt shook his big, distinguished-
looking head and, as Will expected, pulled a cigar out of his inside
jacket pocket. "I've convinced you of that, haven't I?" he said, and
then went to work at lighting it.

"Maybe," Will said. "I mean, I guess so."

The picture of himself and the other kids leaning out of the
bus windows, chanting at the Japanese in their work truck, was

suddenly right in front of his eyes.

"Don't let anybody tell you that just because some of them—the Nisei, they call themselves—are American citizens, that we can trust them. They're only technically Americans because they were born here, but I'll tell you something." He began to chew. "A viper is a viper, whether the egg's laid in Japan or California."

"How come you call 'em vipers?" Will said. "I never heard of them doing anything bad out in California—"

"Precisely."

Mr. DeWitt nodded and chewed as if he had just made everything perfectly clear. Will stirred out of his blue funk and cocked his head at him.

"Precisely what?" Will said.

"The very fact that no sabotage by the Japanese in America has taken place to date is an indication that sabotage is yet to come—if we don't keep them safely locked away."

"I don't get it—"

"California was like the deck of a warship, son," Mr. DeWitt said. "Everyone had to prove that he had a good reason to be there. None of the Japs—American or otherwise—could prove that, so we packed them up, lock, stock, and barrel, and got them away from there."

"That just doesn't sound fair—"

"It was absolutely fair. Every one of them was treated the same." He stuck his cigar into a corner of his mouth and reached out a hand to pat Will on the head. "You're a good boy and you have a big heart—but save it for your own kind. There are enough of them that need it."

Will didn't hear the rest of what Mr. DeWitt said as he finished his cigar and went on to his car. He was more confused than ever.

After that conversation, it was hard to know what to think about more—how to feel about the Japanese living right there in

Santa Fe or how to get Herb to be friends with him again. When he got to social studies class on Monday, it looked like he wasn't going to have much choice about *that*. Herb glared at him over the top of his textbook and wouldn't even say hello. Still, Will went to the Plaza on his bike that afternoon after school and waited until the bells rang from St. Francis Cathedral, but Herb never showed up. Will dragged himself home and just picked at his cabbage soup under Fawn's impatient eye before he asked to be excused to his room.

Even when Mom poked her head in later to say good night, he could barely work up a smile.

"Anything bothering you, son?" Mom said.

"Yeah," Will said. "But I don't wanna talk about it, okay?"

"Of course it's okay," Mom said. "You're allowed to have some privacy. Just remember I'm here if you need me, though."

"Sure," Will said.

As she closed his bedroom door behind her, he wanted to call her back and blurt the whole thing out to her. But Bud had hinted that he should try to be extra nice to his mom right now, because she had so much to do.

At least I've got that *straight,* he thought.

That didn't help much when the next day he was once again walking the halls at school alone. When he reported to Mr. T.'s office at lunchtime, Mr. T. motioned him to the saddle chair.

"Something wrong?" Will said.

"I don't know," Mr. T. said as he joined him. "Why don't you tell me? Your face is so long you're about to trip over your chin. Anything I can help you with?"

Will fiddled with the saddle horn. "It's just dumb stuff," he said.

"I am an expert at dumb stuff," Mr. T. said. "Life is full of it. Try me."

Will twisted his lips up before he started. "Remember when I told you it was hard being one of the only Anglos here?"

"I sure do."

"Well—I finally made friends with one. Herb Vickers. We were havin' a lot of fun until he met Fawn—that's my little sister, sort of—"

"Uh-huh. And she's a pistol, I hear."

"Yes, sir. Anyway, he didn't like her that much, and he said he wouldn't hang around with me anymore if she had to be there."

"And she has to be there."

"Well, yeah! I can't ditch her. She's family."

Mr. T. nodded thoughtfully as he fingered his string tie. "That shows some real class on your part, Will—that you wouldn't just dump your sister for the only friend you have at school. But I'm wondering—do you have to be with Fawn *all* the time? You know, sometimes we fellas need some time to be just the boys."

"Yeah, but she's like one of the boys. You don't know Fawn."

"I see. But that doesn't sound completely healthy either. How old did you say she was?"

"She's 11."

"Isn't it time she had some other girls to play with?"

Will felt a light dawning on his face. "That's what my mom said!"

"All right—so can't you spend some of your time with Fawn and some with Herb?"

"Sure! Only—" Will sagged. "Herb's probably made other friends by now. He won't even talk to me."

"He's a sulker, that Herb," Mr. T. said. "But I have a feeling he'll get over it. Just wait it out and he'll come back. And when he does, you have a deal to offer him. Only—don't forget to fill Fawn in on it."

"Yeah, or I'll probably get jumped. She's pretty tough."

Mr. T. gave a dry smile. "I guess I'm glad she doesn't go to school here—I've already got my hands full."

It didn't seem like that at all to Will. Mr. T. seemed like he had everything handled just fine. Especially later that day in social studies when Herb came back from the pencil sharpener and stopped by Will's desk to whisper, "You wanna meet today? Ride bikes?"

"Sure," Will said, forgetting all about his promise to watch Abe that afternoon.

"No girls."

"No girls. But I gotta play with Fawn sometimes."

"This is not the social hour, people," Mrs. Rodriguez said.

Will looked up to see her black eyes boring into him. He had visions of his mother hearing the whole story, sending him off to his room—

"Yes, ma'am," Will said. "Sorry. It won't happen again."

"Fine. Just get back to work."

Will watched, not breathing, until he was sure she wasn't going to write a note to send with him down to Mr. T.'s. Behind him, Herb made a kissing sound.

That afternoon, just as he'd promised, Herb met Will at the Plaza, and just as if they'd never missed a day, he had a plan in mind. Will was more than happy to go with it.

"We're goin' up to the Cross of the Martyrs," Herb announced, pointing up and east.

"What's up there—I mean, besides the cross?" Will said.

"You can see the whole town from up there." Herb's eyes took on their gleam. "But *none* of the town can see *us*, if you know what I mean."

Will wasn't sure he did, and he didn't ask. He was just happy to have his friend back.

They rode their bikes double speed up the Paseo de Peralta and then walked them the rest of the way on the winding dirt road.

The cross itself wasn't that interesting as far as Will was concerned. Once you took a look at the big, white structure and read the plaque at the bottom that said it had been dedicated in 1920 in honor of the Franciscan monks who died in the 1680 Pueblo Revolt (when the Pueblo Indians took Santa Fe from the Spanish), there wasn't much else to it.

Besides, there was something lonely and empty about being up there. The sky was an endless blue all the way to the Jemez Mountains and beyond. The faint pine smell and the occasional skittering of a surprised lizard were all there seemed to be of life. It was amazing to Will that anything could grow, and yet the junipers and the fir trees and the piñon pines did—in stark, sharp green against the tan dirt they sprang from. Will could feel the constant dry wind sucking the moisture out of his lips.

Herb, however, had plenty of ideas for jazzing things up.

When a jackrabbit showed up, they chased it for at least a half a mile and then peered down into the hole it dove into, with Herb calling, "Here, bunny, bunny, bunny!"

At the sign of a grouse, they tossed pebbles at it to make it fly, and then doubled over with laughter when it had to constantly land on the ground.

"Stupid bird!" Herb said. "Why doesn't it just fly away?"

"Because it's a grouse," Will told him. "They can't fly too far."

Herb liked that even better, and led the way to nearly running the grouse ragged. They might have done so if Herb hadn't spotted a Rocky Mountain mule deer below and taken off after *it*.

It wasn't the way Will had been taught to treat the valley animals, for sure. He could remember going on hikes with the big boys up at the Los Alamos School when Mom and Dad taught there. They all tiptoed and whispered and kept a respectful distance whenever they caught sight of a critter of any kind.

But it felt so good to be running around with another boy, howling for all they were worth and nudging each other with their elbows. Will tried to tell himself the animals probably didn't mind that much.

They were so engrossed in trying to knock down a grosbeak's nest by throwing hard, round little pinecones at it that Will didn't even notice that it was starting to get dark. Even then, it was more the growling in his stomach that tipped him off to the fact that he was already late for supper.

"Jeepers!" he said. "I've got to get home!"

Herb paused, the last of his stash of pinecones in hand, and grunted.

"What?" Will said.

"You sure are a mama's boy, aren't you?"

"Whatta you mean? I'm no sissy!"

"Sure sounds like it to me. You're always afraid of what your 'mommy' is gonna say. Does she wear army boots or somethin'? Carry a whip around with her?"

"No," Will said. "And I'm not afraid of her. I'm just—"

"Yer just scared."

"Am not!"

"Then show it." Herb narrowed his blue eyes. Even in the half darkness, Will could see them gleaming. "Stay 10 more minutes. Or 'til we get that nest down."

Will paused—just long enough to draw another grunt out of Herb.

"All right!" Will said. He snatched up another pinecone from the ground. "First one to knock it out of the tree wins!"

Herb grinned and wound up for a pitch. Will did, too.

Will's aim was better, but Herb was stronger. His next cone sent the nest flying, and Will had to admit to himself that he was relieved. It was getting darker by the second, and the image of

Mom's frown was growing clearer in his mind than Herb's grin right in front of him.

"See you tomorrow!" he called out over his shoulder as he picked up his bike and half-ran down the hill, kicking up dust in big dry clouds behind him.

"Tomorrow we stay 'til it's *all* the way dark!" Herb called after him.

Then Herb took off in the other direction, toward Palace Avenue, dragging his bike behind him. It was immediately quiet. And dark. And spooky. When a lizard skittered across the path in front of him, Will had to smother a squeal.

You are *a sissy, Will Hutchinson!* he told himself sternly. *Nothing's gonna get you up here!*

He was, in fact, more worried about what was going to 'get him' when he got home, and he began to bump the bike down the hill at a faster clip.

I know I don't deserve Your help right now, God, he prayed, *but could You hurry up and forgive me and get me home before—*
"Aaah!"

There was no time to stifle the scream that escaped from him. Ahead of him, just beyond the hill, a flash of light lit up the dusk and then just as quickly disappeared.

"God?" Will called out. "Is that You?"

He knew he was making no sense, but that didn't stop him from jumping onto his bike and pedaling it furiously down the rocky path.

I'm sorry, God! he thought as he jounced painfully on his bicycle seat. *I'm going home now—see me?*

He never got the question answered. The next rotation of the bike's tires took him over a bigger-than-average rock, and before he could even yell again he was hurtling over the handlebars. He landed with a groan on the rocky ground.

It was a good 15 seconds before Will could get his breath back.

Slowly, he rolled over. He had to see whether that flash of light was real or his imagination.

But as he turned over onto his back, he saw a flashlight. And in its light was the face of a Japanese boy.

Chapter Seven

*T*he thoughts wheeled crazily through Will's mind. *I must have busted my head open or something. This fella looks worried.*

The young man's brow *was* wrinkled in concern, and his eyes searched Will's face in the near-darkness.

But then another thought careened around a corner. *It doesn't matter whether the egg is laid in Japan or California,* Mr. DeWitt had said.

Will sat up with a jerk. "Viper!" he shouted.

The young man sat back on his heels, and now that Will's eyes were adjusting to the darkness, he could see the boy's eyes flashing resentment. It was only then that Will realized he was wearing a knit cap.

You're from the camp! Will wanted to say. But there was no time. The tall boy was up and gone, and this time it was Will who was left in a cloud of dust.

Suddenly it didn't matter how mad Mom was going to be— Will wanted to be safely in his home, getting the chewing out of his life. It had to beat this alien hillside.

Mom was standing on the back porch when Will arrived, hugging a sweater around her. When she saw him toss his bike against the house, her hands went to her hips, and Will knew he was in for it. He didn't even have to see her face in the porch light to know her mouth wasn't twitching toward a smile.

"I'm sorry, Mom," he said before he was even up the steps. "I just lost track of time, and then I fell off my bike—"

"Are you hurt?"

"No," he said—although he half wished he were. That might have postponed the inevitable a little.

"I'm sorry," he said again. "I know you get worried when I'm out past dark and you don't need to be worrying about me on top of everything else you got on your mind. And I'm not just saying that, Mom—I really mean it."

"I'm not the one you should be apologizing to," Mom said.

"Is Fawn mad at me?"

"Of course—but I was thinking more of Abe."

Will felt a pang go right through his chest. "It's Tuesday, isn't it?"

"All day."

The uneasy sensation that he might just throw up any second began to take hold in Will's stomach. "I gotta go call Bud," he said.

Mom didn't move. "Before you do, you'd better figure out what you're going to say to Abe."

Yeah. He was definitely going to upchuck.

"Do you know what happened?"

"Tina tried taking him with her to the hospital, but he got so upset she had to call Bud to stop what he was doing and take Abe home. It definitely didn't make her first day on the job any easier."

"I think I'm gonna be sick," Will said, and he sank to the top step.

Mom sat down beside him. "What were you thinking, Will?" she said. "It isn't like you to just run off like that and forget your promises."

"I was with Herb," Will said miserably. "See, he acted like he didn't want to be friends with me anymore last week and then today when he asked me to go play, I just sorta forgot everything else because I was so happy about that."

"You've known Herb for a week. You've known Abe for months." Mom looked Will hard in the face. "Interesting choice, son."

"So what do I do?" Will said.

"What *can* you do? Apologize tomorrow to everyone you've let down. Make sure you're there Thursday. Oh, and go spend a little time in your room."

This time her mouth did twitch.

Will nodded. "I knew that was coming."

"I didn't want to disappoint you," Mom said. She shook her head. "A half hour ago I was ready to string you up by your thumbs if you showed up alive. But what good would that do?"

"I'd be thumbless," Will said.

"And no closer to being responsible and true to your word. From now on, if you aren't home by supper or you fall short on your obligations, there are going to be serious consequences."

Will didn't ask exactly what that meant. But he did say, "I'm gonna go see Abe tomorrow, instead of waiting 'til Thursday, okay?" before he headed for the back door.

"There's a meatloaf sandwich in the icebox for you," she said. "It's more cornflakes than meat, but it'll fill you up."

Will was climbing the stairs with it, trying not to imagine "serious consequences" when the plate suddenly flew from his hand and his arms were wrenched behind his back.

"Jeepers, Fawn," he said. "You didn't even give me a chance to apologize."

"How'd you know it was me?"

Will gave her a look over his shoulder.

"I'm not letting you go 'til you tell me where you were," she said.

"I was—up at Cross of the Martyrs."

"By yourself?"

"No."

"With that Herb boy?"

"Yeah."

"Traitor!"

"But I'm not gonna play with him every day. I'm gonna play with him some days and you some days."

She loosened her hold on his hands a little. "You promise?"

"Yes. Now could you let me go?"

Instead, her hands tightened. "You promised Bud, too, and we all know what happened to that. How can I believe you?"

Will started to feel sick again. She was right, of course.

"I'll tell you what," he said. "If you'll let me go, we can go up to my room and I'll tell you a secret—about something that happened up there tonight."

"Does Herb know about it?" Fawn said.

"No."

She let go of him. "Sorry about your sandwich," she said. "You want me to make you another one?"

"Nah," Will said as he picked it up from the stairs. "I'm not hungry anyway."

"Then let's go!" she said, and she hauled him to his room.

Below, Mom turned on the radio to Abbott and Costello. Fawn shut the door soundly on it and jumped up onto the bed with Will.

"So what's the secret?" she said. "And this better be good."

Will skipped all the stuff about Herb and cut right to where he had started for home on his bike. The way her eyes widened when he told her about falling and rolling over to see the tall Japanese teenager looking down at him, he was pretty sure the story qualified as "good."

"Jeepers," she said. "Do you think he's a spy?"

"No," Will said. "He's from this camp they have here for Japanese people—in case they turn out to be dangerous or something. I've seen him before. Our bus almost ran over him 'cause he was reading in the street."

"What was he doing reading in the street?"

"I don't know," Will said, trying not to sound impatient. It was best not to get on her bad side at this point.

"This is gonna be *our* secret, right?" she said. "You're not gonna tell that Herb boy, are you?"

Will thought about that—and he realized he had already decided not to share the incident with Herb. He would probably want to chase the Japanese kid down with a load of pinecones.

"No," Will said. "This is just between you and me."

Fawn's big smile filled up the lower half of her face. "Then I guess I'll share my bubble gum with you."

But Will shook his head. "I don't deserve any bubble gum," he said.

Fawn skipped off to get it anyway, and Will stretched out on his bed, the planes hanging motionless on their strings above him. *If that Japanese kid had the chance,* he thought, *would he really try to shoot down one of our planes—or murder us in our beds or something?*

Mr. DeWitt—and Herb—would have said he'd do it in a minute. But there was something about that young man that made Will wonder. Before Will had called him a viper, there had been that look on his face—as if he really cared whether Will were hurt or not.

He rolled over—and there were the Tojos grinning through their big teeth from the wall poster. *They have my dad,* he thought. *They're evil and horrible.*

But was the boy up on the hillside evil? Were those children horrible—the ones in front of Alice's who just seemed to want a chocolate malt, the same as everybody else?

Will closed his eyes so he wouldn't see any of it. Then there was only God, waiting for him to talk.

Help me figure this out, would You, God? he thought. And then he was asleep.

He wasn't sure how much later it was that he heard Fawn's voice, whispering in his ear.

"Wake up, Will!" she was hissing. "Wake up!"

"I told you I didn't want any bubble gum," he mumbled sleepily.

"No, silly! There's somebody outside!"

Will began to come out of his fog and sat halfway up. "Is it the air raid warden?" he said.

"Not unless he just screamed like a little girl."

"Huh?"

Will pulled himself all the way awake and studied Fawn's face. There was no teasing twinkle in her eyes.

"I think it came from the vacant lot," she said. She crawled across the bed to Will's window and tugged it open so she could lean out. "Come here and see if you can hear it."

Will joined her and stuck his head out the window. The Santa Fe night was its usual dead-still, and for a minute Will could hear nothing but silence. He was about to tell Fawn she was letting her imagination run away with her when a sound did whimper its way across the stillness.

"Did you hear that?" Fawn whispered. "It sounds like some kid crying, doesn't it? Before I came in here she was crying really loud."

Will nodded. "We better go tell Mom."

"I was gonna, but she's got her door locked. Why don't we just go down and look for ourselves?"

Because I've had enough walking around in the dark for one night, Will thought. But he looked around for his shoes.

"You never even got in your pajamas," Fawn said, looking at his rumpled clothes. "Good thing. We probably oughta sleep in our clothes every night. You never know what's gonna happen with spies around and stuff."

Will rolled his eyes.

Whether there were spies or not, though, Will's stomach was in knots as he and Fawn crept down the stairs and out the back door. Every shadow slanted its eyes at him, and every shaft of light looked to him like white, grinning teeth.

Fawn, on the other hand, was as perky as if she were going on a class field trip. She was two steps ahead of Will as they slipped past Mom's victory garden and into the vacant lot next door. It had grown knee-high with brown weeds, but Fawn waded right into them. Not wanting to traverse them by himself, Will had nearly caught up to her when they both stopped, and he knew she had heard it, too.

Somebody was definitely crying, and that somebody had to be a kid. The weak little sobs were coming out like hiccups.

"What did I tell you?" Fawn whispered over her shoulder. "Come on."

But she hadn't taken two steps before the sobs stopped as if someone had choked them out. And then came a high-pitched scream that could mean only one thing. That "somebody" was terrified.

✝-✟-✝

Chapter Eight

*F*awn was instantly next to Will, practically climbing up his
sleeve.

"What was that?" she whispered.

"Shhhhhh!" a voice said.

"Was that you?" Fawn whispered.

Will shook his head and tried to hear again over the pounding
of his heart in his ears. There was no more crying, but just beyond
them the tall weeds rustled, and Will peered at them through the
dark. They rustled again and swayed in several directions, and
then they were still.

"Whoever it is," Fawn hissed to Will, "she's over there."

Will nodded. What he was supposed to do beyond that, he had
no idea. It was never a good plan to ram around in the underbrush
around here, what with snakes—but, then, snakes didn't cry out
like little girls—and little girls only cried out when they were hurt
or half scared to death. Could he just leave some kid scared and
crying just because *he* was scared?

No, I can't, Will thought. *I already didn't take care of one scared kid today.*

Although the crying had sounded nothing like Abe's, the thought of his big friend inched Will forward.

"What are you gonna do?" Fawn whispered.

He really wasn't sure, but he shook his head at her as he crouched down and silently separated the weeds like he was parting hair. Little by little he crawled through, trying to be as quiet as he could, with the dim glow of the porch light giving him just enough light to see by. He hoped whoever was in there couldn't see *him.* It might just be some little girl crying, but it didn't hurt to have the element of surprise on his side.

He could sense Fawn following him as he coaxed himself further and further into the weeds. When he stopped dead, she collided head-on with his backside.

"Hey!" she whispered. "Warn me when you're gonna stop!"

There hadn't been time. Suddenly, in front of him in a tiny clearing, there were a boy and a girl. They were both Japanese.

The girl looked even smaller and younger than Fawn, especially as she sat with her legs tucked under her dress and hugged against her. When she saw Will, she gasped and hid her face in her knees, her straight black hair falling forward like panels concealing her face.

Will couldn't tell as much about the boy because he was wearing a baseball cap, but his lips looked trembly and scared—until he tightened them into a line and thrust his chin up at Will.

"Please leave us alone," he said. "We're not hurting anything."

"Whoa!" Fawn said over Will's shoulder. "Should we trust them, Will? I mean—aren't they Japs?"

"Japanese," the boy said. "And we haven't done anything wrong."

"Then why are you hiding?" Fawn said.

The girl, who had yet to say a word, whimpered.

"Hey, is she all right?" Fawn said. "We heard her crying all the way over to our house."

"What do you care?" the boy said.

Will was struck again by how much like an American he sounded. That kid at Alice's had sounded like that, too. In fact—

Will peered more closely. The boy drew back, pulling the girl with him.

"I've seen you before," Will said. "Trying to get a chocolate malt."

The girl whined again, louder this time. The boy put his arm around her.

"So—is she your girlfriend?" Fawn said.

The boy shook his head. "She's my sister."

Fawn poked Will in the side. "You better never try that hugging stuff with me. I'll pound you."

The girl let out yet another whimper.

"So—what's wrong with her—your sister?" Will said. "Why's she bawlin' out here in the middle of the night?"

"You might as well just tell us," Fawn said. "You're spies, aren't you?"

"What?" the boy said.

"Hush up, would you, Fawn?" Will said. "Spies don't cry."

"Maybe that's her disguise!"

Will ignored her and tried to figure out what to do next. He could see they weren't out to hurt anybody—but what *were* they doing out of the camp—and hiding, no less?

Well, duh, he thought suddenly. *Why don't you just ask them? Maybe you oughta search them for weapons first—*

Oh, please—just ask them.

Feeling as if he had a tennis match going on in his brain, Will turned abruptly to the boy. "All right—why don't you just tell us what you're doing here. If it's—you know, okay—then we'll let you go."

The girl peeked out from behind her knees. When Will looked at her, she hid her face in her brother's shirt. The boy was watching Will, chewing on his lower lip, and Will suddenly felt mean and small. They were obviously more frightened themselves than scary to anybody else.

Will folded his arms lazily across his chest and said, "So, you're from the camp, right?"

He tried to make his voice sound friendlier, but the girl still let out a muffled cry from the direction of her brother's shirt.

"We were just sleeping out here, and my sister had a nightmare," the boy said. "Sorry we bothered you."

"Why aren't you sleeping in the camp, though?" Will said.

"Hey!" Fawn said. "They kicked you out of the camp, didn't they?"

"Don't be a moron, Fawn!" Will said. "They don't kick people out of prison!"

"It's not a prison," the boy said.

"Yes, it is, Kenichi. It's an awful place and I hate it there!"

Both Will and Fawn stared at the girl. It was the first time she had spoken, and it was obvious from the way she talked that she was every bit as old as Fawn—and almost as angry as Fawn sometimes got.

"Jeepers," Fawn said. "Did you two run away?"

"No," the girl said. She smeared the tears off of her face, as if they were suddenly an annoyance to her. "We couldn't leave our mom—"

"Shut up, Emi!" The boy—who Will was sure the girl had just called Kenichi—slanted his eyes suspiciously out from under the bill of his cap.

He doesn't trust me any more than I trust him! The thought surprised Will—and it made him look more closely at the two kids. Even in the dark, he could tell that they were shivering. It was always cold at night in New Mexico, even in September.

"So, you're planning to go back to the camp?" Will said.

"Yeah," the boy said, still eyeing Will. "Soon as it gets light and we can see, we'll go back."

"Nobody knows you're gone, do they?" Fawn said.

"No!" The girl her brother had called Emi shook her hair back from her face. "We sneaked out to look for our brother and we got lost and ended up here—"

"Shut *up*, Emi!" Kenichi glared at her. She glared back.

Jeepers, Will thought. *They act like me and Fawn!*

"You can't just go telling everybody all our business," Kenichi said.

"Did your brother escape?" Fawn said.

"We don't know—" Emi started to say. Kenichi put his hand over her mouth.

"He left," Kenichi said, as if he were picking each word carefully. "He does that sometimes. We just want to know where he goes."

"We just wanna make sure he isn't getting in any trouble," Emi said, pushing his hand out of the way.

"Emiko!"

"Well, we are," she said.

"What kinda trouble?" Fawn said, edging closer to Emi.

"*No* kinda trouble!" Kenichi gave his sister another stabbing glare and then turned to Will. "We can find our way back to the camp when it gets light. The only reason we're here is because we got tired and she has to sleep where it's not closed in. She hates being closed in. So if you just won't tell anybody we're here, we'll leave as soon as we can see where we're going."

"Yeah, but it's cold out here," Will said.

"I'll go get some blankets!" Fawn said. And in true Fawn-fashion, she was gone.

"She isn't gonna tell your parents or something, is she?" Kenichi said.

"Are you kidding?" Will shook his head. "She'll probably want to sleep out here with you, for Pete's sake."

Emi giggled. She sounded like a little crystal bell.

Silence fell then, and the three of them stood there, the two boys plucking at the grass and Emi looking from one of them to the other.

"So," Will said finally, "your whole family's in that camp? Even your dad?"

"No," Emi said. "Our dad's in the army—he's overseas somewhere."

Will's heart sped up. "Which army?"

"The U.S. Army!" Kenichi said. "What do you think?"

"But I don't get it," Will said. "They let a Japanese fight in *our* army?"

"It's our army, too!" Kenichi said. His eyes blazed from beneath the ball cap. "He's a Nisei—that's a person with Japanese parents born in America."

A viper is a viper no matter where the egg is laid, Mr. DeWitt had said.

But the two kids in front of him sure didn't look like vipers. They looked like a brother and sister who were cold and scared and confused. They could just as easily have been himself and Fawn. Will shrugged.

"So how come you don't like to be closed in?" he said.

"At the camp—"

"Hush up, Emi."

"Do they keep you in a dungeon or something?" Will said.

"No!" Kenichi said.

"But we aren't allowed to have lights on after nine o'clock," Emi said. "And then it's all dark except for that stupid spotlight— but we're stuck in a little apartment with no windows and I can never see the stars at night. In Los Angeles, I could lie in my bed and see the stars, and I hate it that they won't even let us see the stars—"

Kenichi looked as if he were going to clobber her. Will knew how he felt. Sisters could talk longer than you could listen to them.

"If she wants to see stars," Will said, "you oughta go up to the Cross of the Martyrs next time. It's up there—" He pointed. "I saw another person from—"

"Here you go!" said a very breathless Fawn at his elbow. She held out an entire armload of blankets. Will figured she must have emptied the whole cedar chest.

Fawn handed a Navajo Indian blanket to Emi. She wrapped it around her shoulders and practically purred.

"You take some," Fawn said to Kenichi.

He hesitated for a second, and even when he said, "Thanks," his voice sounded reluctant. Taking two blankets and holding them as if they might turn and snap at him, he added, "But how do we get them back to you in the morning?"

"I got an idea," Will said. "Why don't you just come and sleep in our basement the rest of the night?"

Fawn stared at him. If he could have, he would have stared at himself, too. He had no clue where that idea had come from or how it had gotten out of his mouth.

"Can you see the stars from there?" Emi said.

Kenichi poked her in the ribs and shook his head at her.

"Why not?" she said. "It's cold and I'm scared and they're nice—"

"What about their parents, though?" Kenichi said.

"My dad's in the war, too," Will said.

"And we got the best mom in the world," Fawn said.

"Please, Ken—can't we?" Emi said. Even with the blanket around her, she was still shivering.

"I don't know about this," Kenichi said.

"How about if we promise not to tell our mom?" Fawn said. "Would that make you feel better? You could just get up early and be gone before she even knows you're there."

"I thought you said she was the best mom in the world," Kenichi said.

"Mama Hutchie's the greatest, but sometimes it takes a long time to explain stuff to her and you don't got enough time for that. You could be frozen by that time."

"You won't be frozen," Will said. He rolled his eyes at Kenichi, who rolled his eyes back.

"Can we, please, Kenichi?" Emi said.

I gotta teach Fawn to respect me like that, Will thought. *Huh, that'll be the day.*

He still wasn't sure why he was making the offer or even why he agreed with Fawn that Mom wouldn't have to know. In fact, there was a tug-of-war going on inside his head. But the side that said, *Protect these kids. You'd want somebody to do that for you and Fawn*, was winning at the moment.

"You better hurry up and decide, or it's gonna be daylight and we'll still be standing out here freezing our rear ends off," Will said.

Ken, as Emi had called him, gave Will one more long look. It was obvious he had his own tug-of-war happening.

"All right," he said finally. "But you gotta promise you won't tell your mom. No offense, but I hardly trust any grown-ups except my own mother and father."

"We promise," Fawn said. "Now come on!"

Will would rather she had let him speak for himself, but Ken gave him a look that clearly read: *Sisters. Can't they be a pain in the neck?*

There was no time to make a big deal out of it now anyway. Will jerked his head at Emi and Ken and took off after Fawn, who was already halfway to the house. They followed, and Emi even did her crystal-bell giggle most of the way. Every time Will glanced back at Ken, he rolled his eyes.

The house was dark and quiet when they got there. Fawn tip-toed to Mom's door to make sure she was still asleep, and Will got the flashlight out of the kitchen drawer to lead Ken and Emi down the steps into the basement. He flashed it at the windows that were set level with the driveway.

"You'll be able to see the stars through those if you lie down right here," he said. He sniffed at the musty air. "It's a little smelly down here—"

"Are you kidding?" Emi said. "You should smell what we have to live with. The toilets are always overflowing, and they only cart the garbage away about once a month, it seems like. Plus the food stinks—I hate the way the beans smell—"

"He doesn't wanna hear about all that," Ken said. He looked at Will and even grinned a little. When he smiled, Will thought, he looked like a kid you could like.

"Sure I do," Will said. "I never even knew there *was* a camp 'til that day in front of Alice's Soda Shop."

The grin disappeared at once from Ken's face. His eyes clouded. "I don't want to talk about that day."

"Me neither," Emi said. "It was the first time we got to come into town since we've been here, and everybody was so mean to us. I really wanted some ice cream, too, but—"

"Hush *up*," Ken hissed at her.

She clamped her mouth shut.

Will shuffled his feet. "Uh, so, you want something to eat right now? I could make you some cheese sandwiches."

"I want a cheese sandwich!" Emi said.

"Nah—you might wake up your mother," Ken said.

Emi's face fell so hard Will could practically hear it hitting the floor.

"I can be quiet while I do it," he said. "I'll make 'em while you fix up your beds."

Fawn was coming through the kitchen when he got there. "Her door's still locked," she whispered. "I looked underneath and she doesn't have a light on."

"Yeah, but we better get back to bed soon," Will said. "Soon as we give them these sandwiches."

"I wish we had some meat to give them," Fawn said, plopping the slice of cheese Will handed her onto a piece of bread.

"Listen to you," Will said. "A while ago you thought they were spies. Now you want to feed them steak."

"That was back when I didn't know they were regular kids just like us. Can we at least put some butter on them?"

"Nah, Mom'll notice that," Will said. "She has to count the pats to make it last all week."

"I hate feeding them dumb old cheese sandwiches. Hey—how about some milk?"

"I think it's better than what they're getting at that camp. They said they eat beans that smell bad."

"Yuck." Fawn slapped a piece of bread on top of the cheese and lunged to the refrigerator for the milk bottle. It slipped out of her hand and clattered to the floor, splashing its contents into a puddle. The sound seemed to echo from there to the Plaza. It was the only clumsy thing he had ever seen Fawn do.

"Nice work, Fawn," Will whispered. "Wake Mom up, why don'tcha?"

They both got still and listened. There wasn't a sound from the direction of Mom's bedroom. Just to be on the safe side, Will snatched up both sandwiches and dashed toward the basement with Fawn on his heels. When they got down there, Emi and Kenichi were huddled together on one blanket, eyes round.

"What was that noise?" Kenichi said. "You didn't wake up your mom, did you?"

"Nah," Fawn said. "She slept right through it."

"Yeah, but just in case, we better go to bed," Will said. "I'll wake you up at sunrise."

"I'll come down, too," Fawn said. "You wake me up, Will."

"Yeah, yeah," Will said as he steered her toward the basement steps.

He and Ken exchanged eye rolls again, and then Will snapped off the flashlight and felt his way up the stairs, pushing Fawn ahead of him so she wouldn't be tempted to stop and begin another conversation with Emi.

But when she pushed the door open into the kitchen, she did stop, and it didn't take Will more than an instant to see why.

Mom was standing there, arms folded across her bathrobe. "What's going on, you two?" she said.

Chapter Nine

*W*ill couldn't think of a thing to say except, "Hi, Mom."

Fawn evidently couldn't even think of that much. She darted out from behind Will and made a beeline for the back door. The grouse Will and Herb had chased that afternoon hadn't moved that fast—or looked that scared.

"Come back here, Fawn," Mom said without even raising her voice.

Whether Fawn would have or not, they never got to find out. Fawn's next step put her right in the middle of the milk puddle. First one foot and then the other slid out from under her, and she grabbed for the table. Her hand didn't touch it. Her head did, banging so hard that the salt and pepper shakers jittered. It was only the second clumsy thing Will had ever seen her do.

The next few minutes were a confused tangle of questions that never got answered—

"Fawn, what on earth?"

"Why didn't you clean that up, Fawn?"

"What in the world did she slip on? And what are you two doing up at this hour anyway?"

But there wasn't a word from Fawn. There was only a sound that one seldom heard coming out of her mouth. She was crying.

Mom immediately fell to her knees beside her. "Are you hurt, hon?" she said.

That question didn't require an answer. When Will joined his mother, he could see that there was blood trailing down Fawn's forehead from a gaping gash.

"I think I broke my head!" Fawn cried.

"Let me see," Mom said.

"It hurts!"

"I know—let me see what's going on."

Mom's voice was calm, but Will could see the fear flickering through her eyes. He held his breath as she peered at Fawn's forehead.

"It's broken!" Fawn wailed.

"It's not broken," Mom said. "This head is too hard to get broken by something so innocent as my kitchen table. Check that table, would you, Will? Make sure she didn't put a dent in it."

Fawn's crying weakened to a whimper.

"Nah, the table's not too bad," Will said.

"It definitely got its licks in," Mom said. "That cut's going to need stitches."

Fawn started winding up again, but Mom put her hands on both sides of Fawn's face. "Do you really think I'm going to let anybody hurt you? I'll be right there beside you, but you have to stay calm." She turned to Will. "Call Bud," she said. "I'll need him to take us to the hospital. It's times like this I am so furious with myself for wrecking our car."

Will was glad for an excuse to get up. The sight of all that blood was making him feel like he needed a hospital himself. His insides were shaking so hard that it was only after Mom and Fawn were gone with Bud, Fawn's head wrapped in a dish towel, that Will even thought about Ken and Emiko in the basement. He opened the basement door and listened. There wasn't a sound.

They gotta be tired to sleep through all that, he thought. He was, in fact, exhausted himself. The stairs looked like Mount Everest to him at this point. He stretched out on the sofa in the living room, one ear tuned for Bud's car bringing them back, but he didn't fall asleep for a while. The tug-of-war started again, only this time he called God in to referee.

Fawn wouldn't have gotten hurt if we hadn't been trying to hide something from Mom, God, he thought.

But we were just trying to help those kids, just like we'd need somebody to help us. You want us to do that for people, right?

But isn't this against the law?

But the law seems pretty stupid right now—

And, God, should I be trusting anything that involves the Japanese? Can You tell me that?

It was no use waiting for some voice to boom down from the sky. But Will did know from experience that the answer would come from someplace. It was a cinch it wasn't going to come through Fawn! Or Herb—definitely not.

I guess it's gotta be a grown-up, he thought. *I should tell Mom.*

But, he remembered, Kenichi had asked him not to, and even Mom had told him he had to be true to his word. *I just hope I didn't give the wrong "word,"* Will thought.

He fell asleep with the image in his mind of every adult he knew standing before him like they were in a lineup. Unfortunately, nobody stepped forward with an answer.

When he woke up, the first light of morning was coming fuzzily through the front door. He sat up to see Bud carrying in a motionless Fawn.

"Is she unconscious?" Will said, scrambling up.

"No," Mom said. "Just a little dopey. They had to sedate her to get the stitches done."

Bud grinned. "She fought like a wildcat."

"But then, that shouldn't surprise you." Mom's mouth twitched, and Will felt better. If she was almost smiling, it couldn't be too bad.

"Where do you want this?" Bud said, nodding at Fawn whose bandaged head was lolling over his arm.

"Up to her room," Mom said. "And I think I'll crawl in beside her. This has been the weirdest night ever. I even went to bed early and tried locking my door so these two scalawags wouldn't be in there every two minutes asking where's this and can we do that. But then I had all these dreams about people going in and out of the house—it was like a Marx Brothers comedy." Her eyes rested on Will. "But I didn't dream up you and Fawn emerging from the basement at 2:00 A.M. looking like a pair of cats that had just robbed a bird's nest. We *will* discuss that later."

She yawned and followed Bud to the stairs. "Get some more sleep, Will. You don't really have to be up for two more hours."

Will nodded and then forced himself to wait until he heard Fawn's bedroom door close and Bud drive off before he tiptoed to the basement door and listened once again. It was still stone-silent down there, but if Ken and Emiko didn't get moving, he wasn't sure what would happen back at the camp. Their own mom could be looking for them at this very moment.

Checking once again to make sure there was no sound from upstairs, Will crept down the steps and made his way over to the little pile of blankets.

But when he got there, that was all there was: four blankets, but no Emiko and Kenichi. Heart nearly in his throat, Will raced up the steps and out the back door. There was no sign of either of them—not even so much as a footprint.

I hope they're all right, one side of his brain said.

What do you care, really? They're Japanese, the other side tugged back.

Talk to a grown-up about it, the first side said, pulling just as hard in the other direction.

But who?

The lineup reappeared, but still no one stepped forward, and the tug-of-war continued as he got himself dressed while Mom and Fawn slept. The thoughts pulled back and forth, all the way to school, all through his classes, and in the office during lunch. The fact that Mr. T. was behind closed doors with one kid the whole period didn't help much. Will had forgotten to put Mr. T. in his imaginary lineup, but he did seem like a likely candidate. So did Bud, actually, but Will hadn't had a chance to apologize to him yet for forgetting to watch Abe, and he wasn't sure if Bud would want to help him after he'd let down Abe, of all people. Abe was practically his kid—

And so the tug-of-war kept on, even when he was with Herb between classes. Will just let him do all the talking when they were together, which didn't seem to bother Herb that much. Will was still going back and forth during social studies class when he was suddenly aware that Mrs. Rodriguez was calling his name and that Herb was poking him in the back.

"Yes, ma'am?" Will said. He blinked furiously to get the lineup out of his mind.

"I thought surely you'd have something to say on this topic," Mrs. Rodriguez said. She put her square hands on her hips.

"Um, what topic?" Will said.

Mrs. Rodriguez looked more surprised than annoyed.

"Pay attention, please," she said. She gave him a hard look, and Will braced himself for the lecture. But it was his turn to look surprised when she moved on to someone else.

Although he breathed a sigh of relief, Will thought, *That's it. I gotta get this figured out before I get in even more trouble.*

*Maybe if I apologize to Bud and Abe—like I planned to anyway—
I could ask Bud what he thinks.*

He looked up to find Mrs. Rodriguez watching him. Yeah, he
had to get this figured out.

It was perfect that he'd already decided to go see Abe today
instead of waiting until Thursday, so he'd be seeing Abe and Bud
anyway. But that plan seemed doomed from the beginning. He
was heading out the front door of the school at the end of the day
when Herb caught up to him.

"Hey, are we playin' today?" he said.

"Uh—no, I can't today," Will said.

Herb frowned his freckles into folds. "You gotta play with your
sister?" He said "sister" as if he were saying "nose snot"—or "Jap."

"No," Will said. "There's just something else I gotta do."

"Like what?" Herb said.

"There's another kid—my pastor's kid—" Will said. "But we
can ride bikes—uh—Friday, if you want."

Herb's face fell into a sulk. "I thought we were best friends.
We are, aren't we?"

"Sure," Will said. "I guess. I said we could play Friday."

"Maybe," Herb said. "But then, maybe I'll have something else
to do myself."

Then he swaggered off, swinging his lunch pail. Will didn't
have time to worry about it. He hurried down Grant Street to the
Kates's house.

When he got there, a sign was taped to the screen door. For a
crazy moment, Will wondered if it said, "No Japs."

But it read, *Parishioners: Pastor Bud is sick today. Please do
not disturb unless it's an emergency. Thanks, Tina Kates.*

Will didn't realize, until he was on his way back to the school
to see if the bus had left, just how much he'd wanted to talk to
Bud and Abe. Now that he *couldn't* talk to them, Will was almost
certain Bud had the answers.

To make matters worse, the bus was pulling away just when Will got back to the school. Now he was going to have to walk home. Suddenly, that sounded about equal to climbing the Jemez Mountains, and it would get him just about as close to the answer he needed.

Why is this nagging at me so bad? he thought as he trudged back down Grant Street. That was one question that had an easy answer: It was on his mind because he'd met Emi and Kenichi and talked to them and let them sleep in his house. They were practically friends, and he had to know if that was okay. Almost as much, he wanted to know if it was fair for them to be living in camps, almost like prisoners—and eating smelly beans. If only he could just go there and see the camp—

He stopped dead on the corner of Grant and Marcy streets. *What if I did go there?* he thought. *Just to see it from the outside?*

Because you don't know where it is, moron! he answered himself.

But there was always the Cross of the Martyrs. Hadn't Herb said you could see the whole town from up there? He hadn't really paid much attention to that the day before, but if he really looked, wouldn't a prison camp be easy to pick out from the adobe houses and mission churches?

It had to be worth a try. Will looked down Marcy Street. The cross was straight down that way to Ortero and up the hill. When he got that far, it would be even easier without his bike. He didn't give himself a chance to change his mind. He left the corner behind him in leaps and bounds.

There was a briskness to the air that afternoon, and it was drying out his mouth, leaving a crusty trail on his lips by the time he got halfway up the hill to the cross, and he had to slow to a walk. He stopped to wipe at his mouth with the back of his hand.

"So—you had something else to do, huh?" said a voice behind him.

Will whirled around. Herb stood there, arms folded, eyes narrowed.

"What are you doing here?" Will said.

"Following you," Herb said. "How come you walked? How come you didn't bring your bike if you were gonna ditch me? It was too easy keeping up with you."

"I wasn't trying to ditch you!" Will said. "I didn't even know I was coming up here 'til just a little while ago—"

"Huh? I thought you said you had to do something with your pastor's kid."

"I was gonna, but then—oh, forget it."

"Look, you wanna be friends or not?" Herb said.

"Yeah!"

"Okay—then tell me what you're doing up here."

The tug-of-war started again.

Herb hates the Japanese. He's not gonna be any help.

Yeah, but if I tell him to get lost, he might stay lost. I wanna have a friend at school.

"Well?" Herb said. His freckles were folding.

"I was gonna try to find the Japanese camp," Will blurted out.

Herb's face creased into the biggest smile Will had seen on it so far. "Why didn'tcha say so? I know where it is."

"You do?"

"Sure—come on! I shoulda thoughta this myself!"

Without waiting for an answer, Herb took the remainder of the hill in long strides, sending startled lizards scattering for their lives in various directions. When Will reached the top, Herb was already pointing off to the northeast.

"See that?" Herb said, nearly licking his chops. "Look at all that barbed wire—and y'see that tower-lookin' thing?"

"Yeah," Will said.

"That's where the guard stands, 24 hours a day. If one of them tries to break out, he's got orders to shoot at them!"

Will's heart stopped about midway up his throat. "How do you know that?" he said.

"Everybody knows that," Herb said. He shrugged his stocky shoulders. "What else would they do, just let the Japs go so they can do who-knows-what?"

Will didn't look at him. "I don't know. I mean, it's not like a prison exactly."

"Huh!" Herb said. "Who told you that?"

"Nobody!" Will said.

"So—you wanna go down and see it?"

Will finally did look at him—with his mouth wide open.

"I know the way down," Herb said, puffing out his chest. "We can look right through the barbed wire."

"Have you done that before?" Will said.

"No," Herb said. "But my dad always says, 'There's no time like now.'"

Then with a grin that gleamed even in his eyes, Herb bounded down the hill on the other side. Will followed him—but he knew he wasn't gleaming at all.

Chapter Ten

*O*nce Herb and Will got down the hill, they seemed to walk for a long time across flat, treeless ground before they came to the first barbed-wire fence. Will thought of Emiko and Ken hurrying across there in the dark, and he shivered. They must have wanted to find their brother badly—especially to risk being shot at by guards in towers.

But the people Will saw on the other side of the fence weren't looking over their shoulders at the sentries in the guard tower, which Herb pointed out right away as being "pretty swell." Will found himself looking for Ken and Emi among those going about their business on the ground. He saw one dark-haired, round-faced woman pulling a red toy wagon loaded with a pile of laundry. Some men were sitting in the entrances to what looked like chicken coops covered with tar paper. There was one man building a table in front of one of the "coops," and at another there was a woman sewing something, looking up now and then at three small children playing in the dust nearby. Everyone looked busy—

but no one looked happy. And every one of them wore a large tag with numbers on it.

"I'd hate to have to wear one of those all the time," Will said under his breath. "I'd feel like a dog or something."

"They gotta do that, though," Herb said. "How else are they gonna tell them apart? They all look alike."

Will had been talking more to himself than to Herb. Now he wished he'd kept his mouth shut altogether.

This was a stupid idea, Will thought. *I'm just as confused as ever.*

"I've seen enough," he said. "Let's go."

He turned to leave, but Herb put out his arm. "Wait a minute," he said. "There's some kids."

Will looked where he pointed. The door to a building not much larger than the "chicken coops" had opened, and a handful of kids their age and younger were pouring out, just the way the kids at Harrington Junior High burst through the front doors every day when the last bell rang. Some of them scattered to the coops, but most of them headed straight for an open field, which Will now saw had been marked out like a small baseball diamond.

"Hey, you wanna have some fun?" Herb said.

He seemed to assume Will did and sprinted along the barbed-wire fence in the direction of the field.

I'm not so sure about your kind of fun right now, Will thought.

"So are you comin' or not?" Herb said over his shoulder.

"I guess," Will said. But his feet felt heavy as he followed.

Herb stopped when he reached the baseball diamond and gave Will a nudge. "Look at them," he said. "They stole baseball from us."

"What do you mean?" Will said.

"Everybody knows baseball is an American game. I don't know where they get off thinkin' they can play it."

Will looked past Herb to the Japanese kids, who appeared to be choosing up teams. One of them was swinging a bat, and two others were tossing a ball back and forth. It looked to Will like they knew how to play it pretty well. He was about to say that to Herb when he saw them—Emiko and Kenichi.

Emi was swinging her foot back and forth and looking up through her panels of hair as she waited to be picked. Ken was already behind one of the captains, murmuring in his ear as their next choice came up. It looked just like a scene from Will's own school yard. Except that his school yard didn't have barbed wire around it, and it wasn't supervised by army sentries with guns.

They gotta feel so ashamed, Will thought. *They must feel like prisoners even when they're just playin'.*

Right then, one thing was very certain in his mind, and no argument could tug it away: He didn't want Emi and Ken to see *him* watching them like they were animals in a barbed-wire cage.

"I'm gonna go," Will said to Herb.

"Naw," Herb said. "You haven't seen the best part yet." He grabbed Will's hand and put a broken piece of rock into it.

"What's this for?" Will said.

Herb gave him a gleaming grin and showed him the even bigger chunk he was holding. "Watch."

Herb pulled back one stocky arm and hurled the rock, over the barbed wire and straight into the baseball field. A boy still waiting to be chosen for a team let out a yelp as it grazed his shoulder. Black, silky-haired heads whipped around. Dark, startled eyes looked at them.

"That's the way to pitch, Japs!" Herb shouted at them. "Wanna see it again?" He gleamed a grin over at Will. "Show 'em, Will!"

But Will was frozen in place, the rock still clutched in his hand.

"Throw it," Herb hissed. "You got great aim—get that one in the striped shirt."

Will didn't move. But he did look at the boy in the striped shirt, because the boy was Ken, and he was looking right back at Will.

Will came to life. "No, Ken!" he shouted. "I wasn't gonna throw it! See—I dropped it!"

The rock fell to the ground with a thud, but the cold hate in Ken's eyes didn't change. He grabbed Emi by the arm and moved away, but he never took his eyes off of Will.

"What are you waitin' for?" Herb said.

Will didn't answer. He watched until Ken and Emi disappeared behind a set of "coops." Then he himself stalked off.

"Hey!" Herb called after him. "Are you a Jap-lover or what? Hey—if you're a Jap-lover, I'm not gonna be your best friend!"

As far as Will knew, Herb kept yelling until Will was out of sight—and that didn't take long. Will broke into a run that made his side feel like it was splitting open and his chest ache from gasping for air. But nothing hurt as much as the memory of Emi and Ken's faces when they'd thought he was going to throw a rock at them. When they'd thought he was a liar. When they'd thought he was a "Jap-hater."

The bells at St. Francis Cathedral were just beginning their five o'clock ringing when Will finally reached Canyon Road. He was so deep in miserable thought he didn't see what was in the driveway until he was almost on top of it. There was his mother, sitting astride a bright red motorcycle with Fawn right behind her, head bandage and all.

"Look at our new toy, Will!" Fawn said. "Isn't it the best?"

"It's not a toy," Mom said—but her mouth was twitching more than usual. "This is for transportation—it's a necessity around here, especially with you kids forever banging yourselves up." She looked down at the shiny handlebars and then back up at Will. Her eyes were bright. "But it *is* pretty fun-looking, isn't it, Will?"

Will could only stare at it. "You mean this is ours?" he said finally.

"Yep. You know there isn't a car to be had with everything going for the war effort—but one of the doctors at the hospital told me last night that if I really needed wheels, I could probably pick up one of these at this shop he knew about."

"I wanna go for a ride!" Fawn said.

"Not until that head heals up," Mom said. "I'm not too steady on it yet, and I'd like to see you have one set of stitches taken out before they have to put any more in."

"Does Will get to ride it with you?" Fawn said.

"Yes."

"No fair!"

"Will doesn't try to run away when he gets caught red-handed making cheese sandwiches in the middle of the night, so Will doesn't plow into tables and require 10 stitches. Come on, Will, hop on. I'll take you for a spin."

But Will shook his head. "I don't feel like it right now."

Mom gave him a long look. "You two really *are* loyal to each other, aren't you?"

"What two?" Fawn said.

"You and Will. He's not going for a ride because you can't." She twitched her mouth at Fawn. "I'm sure you'd do the same for him."

Will couldn't even look at Mom. *I'm not loyal at all!* he wanted to tell her. *I'm hurting people all over the place and I can't even help it. I don't know what I'm supposed to do!*

He was glad that because Fawn was still healing, Mom made her go to bed right after supper. She tried to whisper questions about Emi and Ken to him every time Mom left the table to go to the stove or the icebox, but Will pretended not to understand her. He didn't want to have to tell her what had happened at the camp, and besides, once she was off to bed—pouting—it was easier for him to hole up in his room and try to sort things out. God was there, of course, as Will stared up at his airplanes.

I don't even know Emi and Ken, but I don't think they deserve bein' locked up like they are—even if it is *their people that have my dad. Emi and Ken aren't Tojos, God!*

But would the government put them there if they weren't dangerous? Ken's eyes were scary-looking when he thought I was gonna throw a rock at them. I just don't know enough, God.

Then it occurred to him that he hadn't followed the last piece of advice God had brought to mind: He hadn't talked to a grown-up about it. He tried to imagine the lineup again—only this time, Mr. T. was the only one who was even in it.

The next day, Thursday, at lunch, the office was quieter than usual. Only one kid came in to see Mr. T., and only because he'd lost his lunch money. When he'd left, quarter in hand, Will slipped into Mr. T.'s office and cleared his throat.

"I was hoping you'd come in," Mr. T. said. "If you hold in whatever's on your mind for one more minute, I suspect your head's going to explode. Have a seat."

Will occupied his usual saddle-chair as Mr. T. sat on his, leaning back and fingering his string tie.

"What's bothering you?" Mr. T. said. "Mrs. Rodriguez says you haven't cross-examined her in several days, so something's going on."

"I've just been thinking," Will said.

"About?"

Will hesitated. Did he really want Mr. T. to know he'd gone to the camp? Nah—there had to be another way to get his answers.

Mr. T. was waiting patiently.

"Do you know anything about that Japanese camp they have here?" Will said.

Mr. T.'s eyes squinted hard lines into his face. "Yes, I do," he said. "And I'm not very happy about it. Matter of fact, Will, there's nothing that makes me angrier right now than that camp."

"You don't think it should be here?" Will said.

"I don't think it should be anywhere! What do you know about it already?"

"Not much—just what Mr. DeWitt told me. He's that banker—"

"I know who he is—he's on the school board, too," Mr. T. said. "And I'm glad you came to me with this. I'd be willing to bet whatever Mr. DeWitt told you was twisted by his bias."

"What does that mean?"

"It means he hates the Japanese—all of them—and whatever he says about them reflects that."

"And you don't hate them?" Will said.

"Hate is a dangerous word. It certainly saddens me that some Japanese people are out there tearing up the world—but to hate them as a race—that goes against everything I believe in."

It sounded like there was a sermon in the near future. Will glanced nervously at the clock. "So—would you tell me the truth about the camp?" he said.

"I'll tell you what I know. Right now there are about 125,000 Japanese people in camps like the one here. They're 'interned,' as they say. Do you know how many 125,000 is?"

Will shook his head.

"That's five times as many people as there are living in Santa Fe. Most of them were living before in places along the Pacific coast—California, Oregon, Washington. And most of them are Nisei—"

"I know what that is. Japanese people born in America."

"Right. And those who were born in Japan and came here to live are called Issei. There's a law that says that the Issei aren't allowed to become American citizens. Anyway, a lot of people in those coastal states have always disliked the Japanese because they claim they've taken their jobs. The truth is, most of the Issei and the Nisei have built up their own businesses—like fishing and farming—because few American companies will hire them. There was a lot of Japanese-hating going on long before the war. The attack on Pearl Harbor just gave them an excuse to get rid of them."

"So they just sent them off to these camps?" Will said.

"Not at first. In the beginning the government just took all the Japanese men they thought might still be loyal to Japan in for questioning. That was disappointing for them, though, because they didn't find a single one they could actually charge with disloyalty to the United States. But they still wanted them out of their communities, and it got pretty ugly. Fear spreads faster than a poison ivy rash."

"So then what happened?"

"At first they asked for volunteers, and a lot of the Issei—and even some Nisei—were willing to move someplace else. The problem was, there were no other communities that wanted them. They'd go someplace like Idaho and they'd find signs saying, 'Whites only. Move on, Japs.' "

"More poison ivy rash," Will said.

"The radio broadcasters and the newspaper people weren't helping. They tended to confuse the enemy nation of Japan with the American citizens of Japanese ancestry. And you know how people are—if they hear it on the radio or read it in the paper, they think it's the gospel truth. And, of course, when all this was going on, Japan was winning one battle after another in the Pacific."

"I know all about that," Will said. "But what's that got to do with, like, kids who are Americans?"

"Absolutely nothing. But the scuttlebutt was that Japan might try to invade the west coast of the United States, and maybe the Issei and the Nisei who lived there would aid the invasion." Mr. T. shook his white-haired head. "There were all kinds of crazy rumors—somebody reported that Nisei farmers in California had planted crops in the shape of arrows pointed at Pearl Harbor—somebody else said they were sending signals to the Japanese from their fishing boats."

"Nuh-uh! Who would believe something like that?"

"Evidently a lot of people. There were the ones who never wanted the Japanese here in the first place, and then there were the ones who just panicked. There was a lot of hysteria going on right after Pearl Harbor."

"So it was California that said they had to go to camps."

"Oh, no—it was the president."

"Roosevelt?"

"The very same. In '42, FDR signed Executive Order 9102—War Relocation Authority. It said all people of Japanese ancestry who were living in any areas in the Western states that were considered militarily risky would have to be 'relocated' to supervised 'camps' located well away from those areas. And do you know what those 'areas' were, Will?"

Will shook his head.

"Anyplace near an airport, a railroad track, a power station, a dam, a body of water. And those people who were making those decisions—members of anti-Japanese groups, all of them—claimed that it was no coincidence that Japanese farms were always located in those areas. Well, no kidding! Wouldn't you want your farm to be close to some form of transportation for getting your goods to market?"

Again, Will could only nod. Mr. T.'s already tanned face had grown darker, his eyes squintier, his mouth harder. If he ever looked this angry with the students, Will was sure they would never darken his office door without being dragged through in handcuffs.

"I'm certain Mr. DeWitt told you that the relocation camps were a 'military necessity,'" Mr. T. went on. "But let me tell you, they are nothing but the result of hate and hysteria. Nothing good ever comes out of that."

He looked at Will as if he'd just realized he was still there. "But you wanted to hear about our camp here, didn't you?"

Will wasn't sure he still did, but he nodded again.

Mr. T.'s face wrinkled up as if he were in pain. "From what I understand, the military took over the old Civilian Conservation Corps camp and converted it into an internment camp. Now this one's a little different from some of the others. This one's actually run by the Justice Department; it's where they send Issei men they still think might be dangerous. They'll let their wives and children come with them if they want."

Mr. T. grunted. "Big of them, isn't it? I've been there once. I figured since there weren't many children at this one they probably hadn't supplied a teacher, so I thought I'd go out and offer my services for the children in the evenings after I was finished here. The army would have none of it. Whatever schooling their kids get, the Japanese have to take care of themselves. As I understand it, they have a sort of one-room schoolhouse going on."

"Yeah, I think they do," Will said. "I saw some kids coming out—"

He stopped suddenly, and his eyes locked with Mr. T.'s.

"You've been there?" Mr. T. said.

Will nodded down at his lap. "I just wanted to see if it was really so bad."

"And was it?"

"It looked dirty—and boring—and there was all this barbed wire, so it's like they're in prison. I wouldn't want somebody with a gun watching me all the time."

"They *are* in prison, Will," Mr. T. said. He leaned forward and spread out his hand. "Anytime—and I mean *anytime*—innocent people's rights are taken from them, they're imprisoned. And I'll tell you something else: Those who take those rights are in their own prison—a prison of fear that controls everything they do."

He leaned back then and just looked at Will. To Will, it was almost as if he knew Will had something more to tell him—and Will was sure he would have if there hadn't been a tap on the door. Mr. T.'s secretary stuck her head in.

"You have a live one to see you, Mr. T.," she said.

"Can it wait?" Mr. T. said.

"I don't think so. He's already blackened one kid's eye, and I fear for the safety of the furniture out here."

Mr. T. looked apologetically at Will.

"It's all right," Will said.

"We'll talk more tomorrow—and anytime you want," Mr. T. said. "And I mean anytime."

He stood up and put out a hand to shake Will's. Will had just stuck his out in return when the door opened and the secretary shoved a large form into the room. The sight of him left Will's hand hanging in midair.

It was Herb, with blood running out of both nostrils—and a face that appeared to be looking for its next victim.

Chapter Eleven

*W*ill had the urge to hurl himself under Mr. T.'s desk. Herb was about the last person he wanted to see right now.

But when Herb's eyes hit on Will, they slowly began to gleam.

Now I'm more confused than ever! Will thought. *One minute he hates me, the next minute he acts like I was just the person he was looking for—*

But there wasn't any more time to consider that right now. As Will moved toward the door, Mr. T. said to him, "Take Herb into the bathroom and help him wash that blood off, would you? Then make sure he finds his way back here."

"Sure," Will said, jerking his head from Herb to the door.

They were barely out in the hall before Herb was gleaming a grin at him. "You faker!" he said.

"Whatta you mean?"

"All this time you've been pretendin' to be this goody-goody—and now I find out you got sent to the principal again!" He shook his head in disbelief, as if he were talking about how many bravery medals Will had won. "I thought after you got sent down the first day of school, you were tryin' to be teacher's pet." He jabbed Will with his elbow as they pushed through the door into the washroom. "How many times does this make for you?"

Will shrugged. "I don't know," he said.

Herb's gleam grew admiring. "Jeepers—you mean you've been down so many times you've lost count?"

"You better hurry up and wash your face," Will said. "Mr. T. doesn't like to be kept waiting."

"I guess you oughta know," Herb said. He gave his face a quick splash. "So—what's he gonna do to me? I hear he never paddles anybody. What is he—a sissy?"

"Mr. T.'s no sissy," Will said.

"He ever paddled you?"

"No."

"Worse?"

Will thought he saw a tiny birthday-candle-size flame of fear weave its way through the gleam in Herb's eyes. *Huh. Who'd have thought?* Will felt a little gleam come into his own eyes.

"You never know with Mr. T.," he said.

Herb dabbed at his nose with the towel. He looked rather pale behind his freckles. "You're not scared of him at all, are ya?" he said.

"Not much," Will said.

"Huh. You're a whole lot tougher than I thought. So—maybe you weren't bein' chicken yesterday after all." He shoved a husky hand through his hair. "All right—I'm givin' you another chance to be my best friend. Meet me in the Plaza after school."

"Can't," Will said.

"Tomorrow?"

Herb's voice was almost begging, and for a second Will felt a little bad for him, bad enough to let him say, "We'll see."

Herb took a deep breath. "Wish me luck with Mr. Tarantino. I prob'ly don't need it, though. I'm pretty tough myself."

"Sure," Will said.

After he walked Herb back to the office, Will sat on the floor in the hall, leaning against the wall and thinking. It had never occurred to him that Herb was as desperate for a friend as *he* was—maybe even more.

After all, Will thought, *he probably doesn't even have anybody outside of school, not like I got Fawn and Abe—*

Will felt a familiar pang. He still hadn't apologized to Abe or to Bud. What if they didn't forgive him? What if he ended up as lonely as Herb? He shook his head, causing the two kids who passed just then to exchange baffled looks. There was clearly only one thing to do as soon as school was out.

Bud looked pale and puny to Will when he walked into the Kates's living room later that afternoon. His color was always on the cream-of-wheat side as far as Will was concerned, but it looked even milkier than usual because he was sick—and that made Will feel worse.

But Bud smiled at him from his spot on the couch where he was wrapped in a blanket.

"I'd offer you a lemonade," he said, "but I have a feeling you want to make this quick. I know it's eating away at you."

"I'm really sorry!" Will blurted out. "I was just trying to make a friend at my school and I just forgot—"

"Apology accepted," Bud said. "You'll want to talk to Abe, too, of course."

"Yeah," Will said. "Where is he?"

"He's not home from school quite yet, which is good, because I want to talk to you about something."

Will's stomach squirmed. "Did I do something else wrong?"

"I don't think so." Bud patted the sofa for Will to sit down. "But I *am* concerned about you. I know I haven't been as available to you as I once was, now that we have Abe to take care of. But I hope you still know that I'm around for you to talk to when you have questions." He chuckled. "And if anybody ever looked like he had questions, it's you. Your face is one big interrogatory sentence!"

"We haven't gotten to that kind in English yet," Will said.

"It's a question. Come on, now, what's on your mind?"

Will wasn't sure he ever would have said anything if the words hadn't rushed out of his mouth all by themselves. "Are you ever supposed to hate?" he said. "I mean, is it always wrong? Like could there be people I'm supposed to hate, only I don't?"

Bud's eyes bulged ever so slightly, and Will was sure he turned even a shade paler. But he gave one of his boyish chuckles.

"How long do we have for this discussion? Whew! I need at least two weeks to try to answer all that!"

It sounded like they weren't even going to get two minutes. The back door smacked shut, and they could hear Abe trudging across the kitchen floor.

"We *will* talk about this, Will," Bud said soberly. "But right now Abe's going to want your undivided attention. You're all he's talked about since the day you missed being with him. So let me just say this: You've learned 'God is love'—not 'God is hate.' And you've read in the Bible that God doesn't hate anything He's made. To me, it just figures, then, that *we* shouldn't hate any of his creations, either. But," he held up a pudgy finger, "there are some things that *people* have created that are *very* worthy of our hate. The trick is to determine whether a thing is God-made or man-made. There's your answer."

At least a hundred more questions crowded their way into Will's mind, but the door from the kitchen swung open, and Abe was suddenly filling up the doorway. He saw Will, and he stopped, his face uncertain. He didn't move but stood there, rocking back and forth on his heels. A pain went straight through Will's chest.

"Hi," Will said. He swallowed hard. "Um—I came to say I'm really sorry about the other day—and it won't happen again—I won't ever forget again—I promise."

Will didn't even get half the words out before Abe's big cheeks were beaming-red and his smile was spreading almost all the way off his face. He lunged across the room and landed practically in Will's lap.

"I think he forgives you," Bud said.

With at least that straightened out, Will felt a little less like there was an endless tug-of-war going on in his head. That is, until Fawn got hold of him that night. After being home from school for two days and forced to "stay quiet" all that time, she was practically clawing the walls when she stormed into Will's room that night during homework time.

"I'd rather go to that dumb school than stay here all day—it's boring!"

"Poor baby," Will said.

"I should jump you for that," she said, fists punched onto her hips. "But I'm not—only because I been dyin' to hear what happened to—" she glanced back at the closed door, "you-know-who that were in the basement."

Will suddenly took a serious interest in the cover of his science book. "Y'know, I really hafta study. Could we talk about this later?"

"Are you kidding?" Fawn's face nearly narrowed to a point as she marched to the bed like a mad goose. "Will Hutchinson— what are you hiding from me?"

"Nothing," Will said. He flopped the book open and stared at it. "When I woke up, they were gone. That's it."

"I don't believe you," Fawn said, knocking the book closed. "You can't tell a lie to save yourself—and you're gonna *need* to save yourself if you don't start talkin'."

Will stubbornly snapped the book back open and glared at Fawn. He hoped she couldn't see the panic that was tying his tug-of-war rope into a knot. *I can't tell her I went out to the camp without her—I can't tell her Herb made it look like I was about to throw a rock at Ken and Emi. She'd never speak to me again!*

He was sure any second she would stomp out, but to his surprise she sagged onto the corner of the bed. "We're never gonna see them again, are we?" she said.

"I guess not," Will said carefully.

"I liked them—well, I liked her. He was kind of a grouch."

"What do you expect? He practically lives in a cage, for Pete's sake—all surrounded by barbed wire, sleeping in a stupid chicken coop—"

Oops.

"How'd you know all that?" Fawn said. Her face started to come to a point again, and so did her finger as she stabbed it in the air in his direction.

"I learned a lot of stuff from Mr. Tarantino today," Will said quickly. "He's our principal."

"You had to go to the principal?"

Will felt like he was sinking into quicksand. "We were talkin'—and he told me a bunch of stuff about the camp. It's pretty awful—and it's not fair, either."

"But—"

"No, listen—"

Before Fawn could ask him any more questions—or point any more fingers at him—Will launched into a word-for-word report of his conversation with Mr. T. He stopped just before the point where Herb made his entrance. Fawn didn't seem to notice the abrupt halt. She was too busy fuming.

"That's the absolutely worst thing I ever heard in my life!" she said. "That's not fair! They never did nothing to nobody!"

"Anything to anybody."

"Yeah! So what are we gonna do about it?"

"Do?" Will said.

"Yeah. We gotta do *something*. Maybe we could go to that

camp in the middle of the night and let them out—you know, help them escape."

"Right," Will said, rolling his eyes. "With guards in the tower with guns pointed at them?"

Fawn studied his face. "How did you know about that?"

"I told you I was up at Cross of the Martyrs," Will said. "You can see it from up there. Look, Fawn, it's not like lettin' birds out of a cage or somethin'. It's dangerous down there."

"Then come up with some other idea, Will," she said. " 'Cause I can't stop thinking about Emi."

"How am I supposed to think with you in here yakking your head off?"

Fawn stood up. "I'll go—but only if you promise to think up some other way we can help them."

"Sure," Will said.

When she left, he abandoned the science book and flopped backward onto his pillows. Fawn sure didn't have any tug-of-war going on in *her* head about the Nisei—at least not the two Nisei they knew. If he thought about it the way Bud said, she had the right idea. God had made Emi and Ken, so he shouldn't hate them.

"Is that right, God?" he whispered.

He didn't hear an answer. But his head stopped tugging.

The next day, there was something else to think about. It was Friday, and Bud had assured him the day before that he would be going back to work for sure and if he wanted to make up for the day he missed he could come over and be with Abe. When Herb asked him if they were meeting at the Plaza, Will said, "Nope. I'm spendin' time with my pastor's kid."

"You're goin' back on your word!" Herb hissed at him.

"You can come with me," Will said.

"You're doin' sissy stuff. I ain't no sis! You're the sis!"

"Yesterday you said I was tough," Will said.

Herb scowled his freckles flat. "That was yesterday."

I don't think I want a friend that changes his mind about me every 10 seconds, Will thought. But he didn't say it. He just shrugged.

Chapter Twelve

*S*pending time with Abe was actually more fun than Will had expected. They played checkers, ate an entire plate of Tina's oatmeal cookies, and listened to *The Lone Ranger* on the radio.

Abe gurgled the entire time, and Will figured out it was just because he was there.

It isn't very exciting, Will thought, *but at least I'm not scared I'm doin' something wrong the whole time—like I was with Herb.*

That was important to Will. Especially after the scene outside the social studies classroom on Monday.

Will was hurrying down the hall from the office when he spotted Herb in the doorway. He would have slowed down anyway, since he wasn't sure what kind of greeting he was going to get. But the group around Herb made Will slow down even more. The half-Anglo boy in their class, the one with the glasses, was with him, and so were two eighth-grade boys, both of them half-Anglo, half-Hispanic. It was easy to identify them; they had coffee-with-cream colored skin and some of them had blue or green eyes or sandy hair. They were sporting bandages on their foreheads, and the seventh grader was squinting at Herb through the one lens in his glasses that wasn't broken.

"All right, so I was a little tough on you guys last week," Herb was saying when Will got within earshot. "I just wanted to find out who had what it took to hang around with me, you know what I mean?"

The kid with the broken glasses nodded. The other two just grunted.

"But I figure you all got it," Herb went on. "I ended up in almost as bad shape as you, right?"

He was right about that. Herb's eye was black and blue, and his upper lip was still swollen. It was a look he seemed proud of as he swaggered back against the door.

"So—what do you say we do somethin' Saturday—together? I got some great ideas."

"Sure!" the kid with the glasses said. "I've got ideas, too—"

"Yeah, well, maybe," Herb said. "What about you two?"

The other boys looked at each other and then back at Herb. Will suddenly had the urge to holler, *Don't do it! He's only gonna get you in trouble!*

But he didn't—and the bandaged boys slowly nodded. Herb stuck his hand out for them to shake it, and his good eye caught sight of Will. It went down to a slit.

Will looked away and tried to squeeze past him into the room, but Herb moved into the space and gave Will a one-eyed glare.

"I guess you noticed I didn't invite *you*," Herb said.

"So?" Will said.

"So—I guess that means I decided you're a sis after all." He curled his swollen lip at the other three boys. "Don't bother with this fella. He's not tough enough."

"Oh, anybody can see that!" Glasses Boy said.

The other two only grunted as Herb finally stepped aside and Will hurried into the room.

It's bad enough we're not friends anymore, he thought as he sagged miserably into his seat. *I don't wanna hang around with him anyway—but did he have to turn everybody* else *against me, too?*

Evidently so, because by the end of the day, kids Will had never even seen before were brushing up against him in the halls hissing, "Sissy." He was never so glad to see a school day end.

But the empty feeling followed him home, and Mom was in no mood to fill it up. Bud, Abe, and Tina were over for dinner, something that usually gave Mom a lift, but she was pricklier than a porcupine as she slapped macaroni and cheese onto their plates.

"I don't know what's the matter with me tonight," she said. "I know why we're rationing—but if I don't get a pork chop soon, I'm going to turn into a wild boar myself!"

"We can't have that," Bud said. "I tell you what—why don't we forget dinner and fill up on candy at the movies? My treat."

"Now, Bud," Mom said over the enthusiastic squeals of the kids.

"Don't 'now Bud' me," Bud said cheerfully. "I owe you about 12 rounds of treats at this point. Come on, gang, everybody into the car."

"But candy for supper?" Tina said.

"Sounds good to me!" Fawn said. She poked Will with one hand and Abe with the other. "Hurry up, before he changes his mind."

Within half an hour Mom had stuck the macaroni and cheese in the icebox and they were all taking up half a row at the Lensic Theatre, sharing bags of popcorn and passing around boxes of Ju-Ju-Bees. Fitting them into his molars like fillings was one of Will's favorite pastimes, and it was almost making him forget about Herb and Emi and Ken—when the lights went down and the newsreel started.

At once, the big screen was flickering with a shot of American soldiers, an endless line of them, trudging down a dirt road with packs on their backs. Their faces were lined with dirt and with weariness.

As always, Will strained to see if any of them was Dad. But the newsreel announcer's dramatic voice said, "Allied forces continue to make their way across occupied territory and toward possible victory—"

"Victory?" Mom whispered. "They look like they've just been beaten half to death!"

Abruptly, she handed Will the popcorn bag and got out of her seat. She climbed over him and Fawn and Abe and Tina and Bud as if they were pieces of furniture and hurried up the aisle.

"She musta had to go to the bathroom bad," Fawn whispered.

But Will shook his head, and he himself climbed over everyone to go after her. He found her in the lobby, staring vacantly into the candy case. He was pretty sure she wasn't getting more Ju-Ju-Bees.

"Hi, Mom," Will said carefully.

"Go back in, son," she said. "You don't want to miss the cartoon."

But Will didn't move. He had seen her eyes get empty like that several times since the war had started. It was as if the real Mom went away someplace else—and he always hated those times. He definitely didn't want her to go there now.

"That wasn't Dad in the newsreel," he said. "I looked."

She shook her head. "No—but those boys we saw—they're every man that's over there, in Europe or the Pacific. They all looked the same, didn't you see that?"

"Yeah, kinda," Will said.

"It scares me, Will," she said. "I wonder if any of them will ever be able to return to the lives and the thoughts they had before they went over there to fight this rotten war." Her voice was getting thick. "Seeing those soldiers go through that—and knowing that what your father is enduring is probably so much worse. He can't take it, Will. He's too sensitive. He's an artist, not a fighter."

"Dad can do anything, though," Will said. His own voice was getting thick, too—from his heart beating up in his throat.

"But why should he have to?" Mom said. She smacked angrily at the tears that had managed to escape down her cheeks. "Those miserable Japanese! I'm going to the ladies' room."

She darted off. Will found himself staring at his own reflection in the candy case.

"She thinks the Japanese are miserable," he murmured to it. "Maybe that means there are some people we *don't* have common ground with."

"Can I help you?" the girl behind the counter said.

"No," Will said. "I don't think anybody can."

All through that week, Will fought the tug-of-war in his head. Even though Mom seemed to wash away her mood when she washed her face in the movie theater restroom, their conversation stayed stubbornly with him.

One minute he was remembering her fierce words: "Those miserable Japanese."

The next he was hearing Bud say, "Love all of God's creation, but hate the things man does to destroy it."

One minute he was being pulled toward Mr. DeWitt telling him a viper was a viper no matter where it was hatched.

The next he was being hauled back to Mr. T. saying the Nisei were being imprisoned unfairly.

What made it all worse was that the number of people he could talk to was getting smaller.

He didn't dare bring it up with Mom. He didn't want her diving back into a black mood, and besides, she had never pinned him down about why he and Fawn were in the basement that night. He didn't want to remind her.

He thought he had gotten all he could from Bud and Mr. T.

Fawn was out of the question. If he brought it up again, she was sure to corner him about how he knew so much—and then she'd find out about his day at the camp.

It was in social studies one day, of all places, that he came up with a possible new source.

Mrs. Rodriguez opened the class as usual by asking if anyone had any new questions about the war they'd like to bring up. Will was surprised when she called on Herb.

"Yeah, I got a question," Herb said. "How come they let those Japs from that prison camp run all over town?"

The class buzzed, and Will was pretty sure most of them were as in the dark about the camp as he had been. Mrs. Rodriguez shushed the class with a square hand.

"First of all," she said, "I would prefer that we call them 'Japanese,' not 'Japs.'"

"Why?" Herb said.

"Would you like to be called a 'gringo' instead of an 'Anglo'?" Mrs. Rodriguez said.

The Hispanic kids in the class snickered. Will didn't have to turn around to know for sure that Herb's freckles were folding in a frown.

"No," Herb said. "But nobody would call me that because I don't deserve it."

"And you think the Japanese do?"

"Well, yeah. They're the enemy! That's why I don't get why they're allowed to run around loose when they bring 'em into town. My dad says—"

The class never got to find out what Herb's dad said, because just then the air raid siren blew. As always when the horn went off, faces looked momentarily panicked.

"It's only a drill," Mrs. Rodriguez said. "You know what to do."

Quickly and quietly the class filed out into the hall and down the stairs to the basement where they gathered in a knot around Mrs. Rodriguez, just as the other classes were doing around their teachers. Nobody was allowed to say a word, though Herb was saying plenty to Will with his eyes.

You're outa my group, sissy.

When they got back to the room, Mrs. Rodriguez put them to work reading the next chapter in their texts about the unions. As Will hurried through it, he couldn't shake off the idea that was forming in his head.

I never thought of asking Mrs. Rodriguez what she knows about the Japanese and the camp and stuff. Maybe I oughta stay after class and find out how she was gonna answer Herb. Maybe I oughta—

"Maybe" turned into "should," and when the bell rang, Will took his time shoving his book and papers into his book bag. Everybody else was trying to squeeze out through the door as if somebody were handing out malts in the hall—except for Herb and his new friend with the broken glasses. The more slowly Will tried to move, the longer Herb and Glasses Boy lingered.

"Whatta ya waitin' for, sis?" Herb said to Will. "Afraid to go out in the hall with me and my friends?"

Will forced out a laugh. "No," he said. "Why should I be?"

Herb poked Glasses Boy. " 'Cause we're tough, and you're a sis."

Glasses Boy actually looked about as tough as a ball of cotton, but it was enough to stiffen Will from toe to cowlick.

"I'm not afraid of any of you," Will said. And he tossed his book bag carelessly over his shoulder and walked out, past Mrs. Rodriguez and the answers she might have. He was miserable enough as it was. Why stir up even more trouble with Herb?

There were other things to keep him busy. The afternoons with Abe were fun, especially when Fawn joined them. Abe's favorite game was putting both of them on his back and running until all three of them fell, but Mom put the kibosh on that, saying she didn't need to take any more kids to the hospital for stitches. After that, they couldn't pay Abe to do it.

But on Saturday, Will was miserable again. They were in the second half of September by then, and the weather was getting more brisk, so the kids could have run around even more without dropping over from the dry New Mexico heat. But Mom said Fawn had to stay quiet until the doctor totally released her, and Tina wanted to spend time with Abe herself on the weekends. Herb, of course, was out of the question, and that was actually all right with Will. The more he saw him strutting around with his new friends, ordering them around and bullying them into laughing at his not-funny jokes, the more Will was glad that he wasn't one of them.

Still, hanging out alone on a Saturday made the tug-of-war worse than ever. Will was being pulled in the I-don't-know-about-those-Japanese direction that afternoon, and he found himself pelting darts at his Tojo poster when Mom tapped on his door.

"Come in," he said, letting another dart fly.

Mom stood in the doorway for a minute, purse strap over her shoulder, her going-to-town hat perched on her head.

"Do you want me to do something?" he said.

"No," she said. Her eyes went to the poster. "You certainly have good aim."

"It's all right, I guess," Will said. Something in the way she said it made him want to squirm.

"I just wanted to tell you I'm going shopping," she said. "And I'm taking Fawn with me before she climbs the walls." She started to go out, and then she stopped, hand on the doorknob. "Oh, and Will," she said. "Be careful what you're aiming at, all right?"

What do you mean? he wanted to call after her. *Tell me what I'm supposed to think, Mom!*

But he didn't. And then she was gone.

The house got unbearably quiet after that, and Will couldn't stand it any longer. Around three o'clock, he'd thrown darts until his arm ached and there was no sign of Mom and Fawn coming home. Finally, he got on his bike.

At first he rode through town, but there wasn't much going on. The man who never had an expression on his face was sitting at a table at the outdoor café in front of the LaFonda Hotel as usual, working his eyebrows and smoking his pipe. But even wondering about him seemed boring, so Will rode on. He wasn't sure where he was going until he ended up at the Cross of the Martyrs.

He hadn't been there in a couple of weeks, and he was surprised at how different it seemed now. The air was more brisk and clear since fall had finally hit, and the smell of piñon pine logs burning in the fireplaces below was homey. Somehow that made Will sad.

He tried to cheer himself up by picking some pine nuts, but they weren't as good raw as they were when Mom cooked them into casseroles at home. A film of gray clouds was veiling the sun, and a wind was kicking up, drying out Will's mouth and blowing sand into it to boot. That same wind also made a few blue spaces in the sky, but not enough to let many splashes of sun come through that were big enough to sit in. He could find only one, at the top of the hill. He sat down and hugged his knees, and then he shivered anyway. He was right above the Japanese camp.

He thought of moving away so he wouldn't have to see it, but somehow he couldn't. He watched as the tiny figures below moved around inside their barbed wire boundaries.

And I think I'm *bored*, he thought. *They don't have* anything *to do.*

And yet everyone seemed to be busy with something, though from that distance Will didn't know what. He could just see that they kept on living, even though there wasn't much that he could see that was worth living for.

I hope Dad's doing that, he thought suddenly. *I bet he is. I bet he keeps his hands busy. I bet he draws—even if it's just in the dirt. I bet he does! He'll make it—Mom's wrong—he's strong—*

"Hey," said a voice. "You all right?"

In the instant he whirled around to look up, Will realized two things. One was that he was crying. The other was that there was a tall Japanese boy standing right behind him.

Chapter Thirteen

*I*t wasn't just any Japanese teenager. It was the same one the bus had almost hit that day. The one the kids had all yelled at. The one Will himself had called a viper, right here on this hillside.

Will started to scramble up, but the boy put his hand on his shoulder. Will froze, and he knew that if his face gave away what he was feeling inside, it was the picture of fear.

"Well," the boy said, "at least you're not calling me names this time."

His voice wasn't angry, but it wasn't exactly friendly, either. Will shook his head, his heart still pounding crazily in his ears.

The boy let go of Will's shoulder. "I'm not gonna hurt you," he said. "I just wanted to make sure you were all right. Are you hurt?"

"No," Will managed to say. "I'm fine."

The boy nodded and stepped back. "Go on, then," he said. "I'm not stoppin' ya."

His face lost all trace of concern and seemed to harden right before Will's eyes. It reminded him of towels drying stiff on the clothesline in the middle of winter. The young man walked away from Will and dropped lightly to the ground against a pine. He pulled a flashlight out of one pocket and a book out of the other. A pen appeared from still another one.

Will could have run. He was sure he should. But he found himself taking a step toward the boy. He looked up, eyes narrowed.

"What?" he said.

"Is that the book you were reading when the bus almost hit you?" Will said. And then he wanted to bite his tongue in two.

"Were you on that bus?" the boy said, voice tight.

"Yeah," Will said, "but I—"

The boy gave him a hard look and then turned back to the flashlight and began scratching furiously in the book with his pen. Still, Will couldn't leave.

"Are you from the camp?" Will said.

The pen stopped.

"I'm not gonna tell anybody, so don't worry," Will said.

"Yeah, I'm from the camp," the young man said. "What's it to ya?"

"Nothin'. Just tryin' to be friendly." Will swallowed. He wasn't sure why he was trying so hard, but he couldn't seem to stop himself. It suddenly felt like the only way to find out about these Japanese. "I just live down there," he said. "See—that's my house— the white one that looks different from the rest."

He pointed down to Canyon Road and glanced sideways at the Japanese boy. He paused a second and then let his gaze follow Will's pointing finger.

"The others are mostly Spanish pueblo," Will said. "But ours is different, which I guess makes sense since we're different from just about everybody else in town. There aren't many of us Anglos, you know."

"There are enough of you," the young man said. "Your kind gives us more trouble than anybody. *Hakujin.* So if you don't mind—" He nodded at his book and pen.

"What's hakujin?" Will said.

This time the boy didn't look up. "White people," he said. "White people who are strangers to us in a city that isn't our home."

"But I'm not like the rest of the hak—hak—whatever you said. At least, I don't think I am. In fact, one night I even helped two kids from the camp—gave 'em cheese sandwiches and a place to sleep."

"Sure ya did," the boy said. He kept writing.

"Maybe you know 'em," Will said. "Kenichi and Emiko?"

The names had barely left his lips before the Japanese boy was on his feet, and before Will could even move, the boy had him by the shoulders, fingers pressing into Will's skin. His eyes bored into Will's.

"Who did you say? What were their names?"

"Emiko and Kenichi," Will said. "They called each other Emi and Ken." He licked his lips. "I guess this means you know 'em, huh?"

The boy nodded, but only slightly. It wasn't enough to make Will feel any safer, not with the way his narrowed eyes were smoldering.

"Why did you ask me that?" he said.

"Because," Will said.

"You weren't just trying to make conversation." The young man gave Will a shake. "Why did you ask me?"

"Because I want you to give them a message for me!" Will said. It had come from who-knew-where, but it was out there now, and there was no taking it back.

"What message?" the boy said.

Will licked his lips again. They were so dry from fear and the wind, they were sticking together. "Um—I think they think I'm a Jap—I mean a Japanese-hater, and I'm not. Tell them the rock I was holding—I didn't pick it up—that other kid put it in my hand. I was never gonna throw it—honest. Please—tell them that."

By now the Japanese boy's face was within an inch of Will's. He didn't dare breathe.

"You better be telling the truth, kid," the boy said. "Emiko and Kenichi are my brother and sister."

"Oh!" Will said.

"What?" The fingers dug in harder.

"You must be the brother they were talking about. They were out looking for you!"

The boy shook Will again, and then he let go. Will wanted to run this time, but the boy's face froze him to the spot.

"What were they thinking?" he said.

"Well," Will started to say, "I think they were afraid you were gonna run away or something."

"They know better than that! I wouldn't leave them here!" He turned around and threw his hands up in the air. "All I want to do is be where I can see the whole world again—it's the only thing that keeps me alive and hoping."

"You picked the perfect spot then," Will said with a cheerfulness he didn't feel. "You can see the world up here, but the world can't see you; at least that's what one fella told me—"

But the Japanese boy didn't seem to be listening. "I know what I'm doing! I know how to slip through the fence and not get caught—they don't. They can't leave the camp like that again!"

Then without another glance at Will, he stuffed his flashlight and pen and book back into his pockets and disappeared down the hill in a cloud of dust. In a moment, there was only the gathering darkness.

"Jeepers," Will whispered. "I thought *I* got mad sometimes."

But he knew there would be nobody in the world madder than Mom if he didn't get home. Dusk was already falling, and he knew it had to be long past five o'clock.

He was right. He could see Mom and Fawn at the dinner table through the back window as he climbed the back steps, and he prepared himself for the tongue-lashing.

But there was none. Mom merely looked up, her face white and twitchless, and pointed to the stairs.

"Mom, I can explain," Will said—and he really wanted to.

But she shook her head. "You don't want to get into a conversation with me, Will," she said. "Believe me, you don't."

Will was pretty sure if he did, he was going to hear about the 'serious consequences.' He nodded and took off for the stairs.

He lay on his bed for a long time, waiting for Mom to calm down enough to come up and give him the bad news. He heard her and Fawn doing the dishes. He heard Fawn go to her room without even hesitating outside his door. He heard the radio being snapped on and Ernie Pyle's voice talking.

He closed his eyes. *God, when am I ever going to stop messing things up? I try to find common ground. I try not to hate the wrong things. But it keeps winding up that I'm alone. I can't do it—*

Will was close to tears again, just the way he'd been on the hillside—but once again something stopped him. It wasn't a voice behind him this time. It was the sound of something hitting his window.

He got very still and listened. There was silence, and then once more a spattering against the glass as if someone were throwing a handful of stones.

Will scrambled across the bed to the window and peered down. There, peering back up at him through the darkness, was Ken and Emi's brother.

Will shoved the window up and leaned out. The boy motioned

urgently with his hand for Will to come down. Will nodded, but when he rocked back on his bed, he hesitated. Had Fawn heard? Or worse, Mom? Wasn't he in enough trouble already?

He poked his head out the window again. The boy was still there, and at the sight of Will, he looked as if he would jerk his head right off of his neck gesturing at Will. Even in the darkness, Will could tell it wasn't an angry motion. It was an urgent one.

Will nodded at him, backed off the bed, and jammed his feet into his shoes. Grabbing a sweater, he crept soundlessly down the front stairs and paused at the bottom in the doorway to the dining room to listen. Ernie Pyle was still talking, and there wasn't a sound from Mom. Praying that not so much as a board would creak, Will tiptoed to the front door and let himself out.

The boy was nowhere in sight, but when Will darted through the shadows toward the front fence, he popped up and motioned Will over, his head still in emergency mode. Will lifted himself over the fence and crouched down with him.

"Have you see them?" the young man said.

"Who—oh, you mean Emi and Ken? No."

The boy muttered something under his breath.

"They aren't at the camp?" Will said.

"No—why would I be asking you if they were?"

"Then they're probably out looking for you again," Will said.

The boy drove his eyes into Will's face. "Are you always this good at stating the obvious, Hakujin?"

Will didn't know what he meant, but he didn't ask. He just shook his head.

"I thought they might come here again," the boy said.

"I don't think so. They still think I was going to throw rocks at them—and I wasn't, I swear—"

"Shut up!"

Will did.

"Where did you find them before?" the boy said.

Will pointed to the vacant lot.

"Where exactly?"

"You want me to show you?" Will said. The boy's face was so hard, Will didn't dare make a move without asking him first.

"Yeah, show me," the boy said.

With a wary glance back at the house, Will got to his feet and, staying low, ran to the overgrown lot next door. Though they combed through the weeds for 10 minutes, there was no sign of Emi and Ken.

"You said you gave them cheese sandwiches—" the brother said suddenly.

"Yeah—you want one?"

"No, I don't want one! *Where* did you give them to them— here?"

"No, in my basement. But—" Will's stomach went into a knot. "If we go there, my mom might—"

But the boy had already taken off toward the Hutchinsons' house.

If Mom catches him, she's liable to bean him with a frying pan! Will thought. Although at this point that didn't sound like such a bad idea, he was more worried about Emi and Ken than he was scared of their brother. He took off after him.

The boy was peering into one of the basement windows at the front of the house when Will got there, and he shook his head at Will.

"I didn't think they'd just let themselves in," Will whispered.

"I'm not interested in what you think," the boy hissed back. By now his face was so tight and hard, it seemed to stretch his eyes into demon-slits. The look of it made Will's blood run cold.

I don't care how much trouble I get into, he thought. *I'm getting Mom.*

But before he could even turn himself around, something heavy dropped on him, as if a sack of potatoes had been hurled from the second-story window. He had hit the ground before he knew what it was.

"Fawn!" he whispered angrily. "What do you think you're doing?"

She didn't answer, but threw herself at the Japanese boy and pinned him to the ground. His hard face didn't look frightened, but it was clearly surprised.

"All right, spy," Fawn whispered into it. "What's your name—and I mean your real name?"

"Fawn—" Will said.

"Get off me, kid!" the boy hissed.

"Not until you tell us your name, rank, and serial number!"

"Yoji Lin! American citizen. You want my number—read my tag!"

The boy gritted his teeth hard and yanked one of his arms from Fawn's grip. He snatched up the tag that hung from his neck and stuck it into her face. She sat back and blinked.

"Get off him, Fawn!" Will whispered. "He's Emi and Ken's brother!"

Will had never seen Fawn move so fast. She leapt from atop Yoji as if he were sending out an electrical current and grabbed onto his wrists to pull him up. He wrenched himself away and glared at her.

"Sorry," Fawn said. "I wouldn'ta done that if I'd known. Me and Emi—we're friends."

"Oh," Yoji said, brushing leaves from his shirt with a vengeance. "So you don't throw rocks like your pal here?"

"Huh?" Fawn said. "What's he talking about, Will?"

"Never mind," Yoji said. "You haven't seen them, have you?"

Quickly, Will filled her in on Emi and Ken's disappearance. Fawn's eyes grew round with concern—and, Will saw, with a plan.

"Fawn," he said, using his warning tone. "What are you thinking?"

"I'm thinking we have to do something!" she said. "And I know what." She turned to Yoji. "Our mom has a motorcycle. You take that and drive around the outside of town. Will and I will each take half of the inside. They've gotta be somewhere—"

"Fawn, are you nuts?" Will said.

But Yoji apparently liked the idea. "Where's this motorcycle?" he said.

"No—you don't understand!" Will said. "She gets these crazy ideas, but they only lead to trouble—"

"And you don't think my little brother and sister are in trouble already?"

Yoji glared down at Will, eyes glinting from their slits.

"It's in the garage," Will said. "But don't start it up 'til you get to the top of the road."

Yoji nodded and slipped off through the shadows for the garage. Will turned his own glare on Fawn—but it was pointless. She was already headed down Canyon Road, whispering hoarsely over her shoulder, "You take the east side, I'll take the west. And remember—Emi likes to be where she can see the stars."

"You're gonna see stars when I bean you one!" Will whispered back. But, once again, it was no use. He sighed a tormented sigh and headed through the backyard in the direction of Palace Avenue.

But neither Palace Avenue nor the rest of Santa Fe's east side turned up any sign of Kenichi and his little sister. Will was turning into an icicle by the time he finished, and he huddled onto the front steps of St. Francis Cathedral to try to warm up.

It was obvious that running around like a headless chicken wasn't doing any good. That was Fawn for you, he thought—just run off without thinking.

Okay, so think, he told himself. *Where would they go? What do you know about where they'd go?*

It surprised him after a few minutes to realize that he really didn't know very much at all. *But I feel like I know them,* he thought. *Why is that?*

But there wasn't time to wonder about that. The next thought—that Emi and Ken could right now be being dragged back to camp by guards with guns—nudged him to think harder. What was everything—absolutely everything—he did know about them?

They loved their brother.

Ken protected Emi.

Emi had to sleep out where she could see the stars when she woke up or she would have nightmares.

Will studied that. That had to be a clue. They wouldn't be hiding in some cave or tunnel. In fact, he himself had told them to go up to the Cross of the Martyrs if—

Would they do that? Would they remember that?

Only because it was all he had to go on did Will race down the steps two at a time and run with all he had left toward the hill.

Chapter Fourteen

*T*he night wind was whipping sparks from the chimneys and flinging them across the sky like fiery stars as Will raced out of town. *Sparks are gonna be flyin' like that out of Mom's mouth,* Will told himself, *if I don't get back home before she finds out both me* and *Fawn are gone—and also her motorcycle!*

But the thought wasn't enough to drive him back there without at least trying to find Emi and Ken. Whether he really knew them well or not, he had to do this. And it was no longer because he was afraid of their brother.

Night on the hillside leading up to the Cross of the Martyrs was a different story. *That* he was afraid of. It was windy and dark and full of the shadows of the unknown. If Emi and Ken *were* up here, he was sure Emi was whimpering to beat all, even though she could see practically every star in the entire galaxy. It struck him as he climbed, heart pounding, that they must hate white Americans by now as much as the white Americans hated the Nisei.

Some of the white Americans, he corrected himself. *But not me.*

And this time, there was no tug in the other direction.

Even though the wind was whistling eerily through the pines, Will knew before he even reached the cross that Emi, at least, was there. He could hear her whimpering.

When he climbed the last few feet, he could see why. She wasn't even wearing a sweater, and though she cowered against her big brother, she was shivering. Will took off his own sweater. Ken stood up and shook his head.

"We don't need any help from you!" he said.

"No—Kenichi—you're wrong!" Will said. "Here, Emi!"

He tried to hand her his sweater, but Ken snatched it from him and threw it to the ground.

"I'm not what you think!" Will cried. "I'm not a—a hakujin. I'm not!"

Ken froze. "Where did you learn that word?" he said.

"From your brother," Will said.

Emi was on her feet at once. "From Yoji?" she said. "You met Yoji?"

"Emi—shut up," Ken said. But he didn't take his eyes off of Will.

"I did meet him," Will said. He pushed the words out so Ken would hear them all before he stopped him again. "I met him up here, and then he came to my house because he went back to the camp and you weren't there—he's looking for you. He wants you to go back to the camp so you won't get in trouble!"

"Is he running away?" Emi said. She clamped her hands around Will's left one. They were clammy and cold.

"He doesn't know anything," Ken said. "Don't ask him."

"Yes, I do! I do know!" Will said. "He's not running away. He just comes up here sometimes to see the whole world instead of just the camp. He just sits and writes in that book he carries around with him."

"His journal!" Emi said.

Ken hushed her up with a wave of his hand. His eyes narrowed, and for a moment he looked just like the angry Yoji. "Then where is he now?" he said.

"Riding around on my mother's motorcycle looking for you!" Will said. "He wants you to go back to the camp—and he'll come."

"How do we know that?" Ken said.

"Because I'll tell him."

"I don't trust you."

"Oh, shut *up*, Kenichi!"

Both boys stared at Emi. She had her hands on her hips, and for a second Will was sure she was going to jump one of them. It crossed his mind that it was no wonder Fawn liked her so much.

"I believe you," Emi said to Will. "If you say Yoji wants us to go back to the camp, then that's what we should do."

"And how are we supposed to find our way back in the dark?" Ken said.

"It's not that hard to get there from here," Will said. "You just go down this way and—"

"How do we know this isn't a trap? How do we know that friend of yours isn't hiding with a rock to throw at us?"

"He isn't my friend," Will said. "You're more my friend than he is."

"Huh," Ken said. "All right—prove it."

"How?"

"You go down with us—to the camp."

Will's heart stopped. "I can't," he said. "When my mom finds out I'm gone, she'll—"

"That's what I thought," Ken said. "I don't need friends like you. Come on, Emi." He stuck out his hand, and his sister took it. Her face crumpled as she walked past Will, and he could hear her whimpering as she trailed behind Ken, down the hill.

I'd go if I could! Will wanted to shout after them. *But you don't know how much trouble I'm already in. I'll tell Yoji I found you—*

Just below him, Emi stumbled, and so did Will's thoughts. She went down on her knees, whimpering even louder.

"Hey," Will said. He swallowed hard as he picked up his sweater and went toward them. "I better go with you."

Ken opened his mouth, and then he closed it. Emi got to her feet and, to Will's embarrassment, slid her hand into his.

Maybe she's not so much like Fawn after all, he thought.

At least the darkness was good for one thing: It kept Ken from seeing how red Will's face was with a girl holding his hand. Ken's face, on the other hand, stayed stiff and almost-hard.

But even though clouds continued to blow in front of the moon, Will found his way down the hill with surprising ease. Maybe hanging out with Herb had had its good points after all.

The closer they got to the camp, the softer Will's heart beat. It seemed to have the opposite effect on Emi. The nearer they got, the harder she clung to his hand. Even Ken's face went from hard to pinched, and when Will said, "Where did you come out?" he shushed him fiercely.

"Sorry," Will whispered. "Where did you come out?"

Ken nodded his head and took the lead, with Will following and Emi clinging to his arm with both hands. She didn't make a sound, but Will was sure she was whimpering inside.

Ken led them to a spot where the barbed wire turned a corner. The bottom row of wire had been bent so that there was a space just wide enough to crawl through if you were careful. Even at that, Will decided he'd never want to chance it. He had visions of coming out ripped to ribbons. *They must really love their brother,* he thought.

"You first, Emi," Ken whispered.

He squatted and held the wire farther apart from the one above it, but Emi didn't let go of Will's arm. Instead, she turned her frightened face to him and said, "Thank you, Will. I don't care what Kenichi says—you're my friend."

"Yeah, well, all right," Will said.

"Come on, Emi, hurry up," Ken said.

For once Will was grateful for Ken's cutting in. He pried his arm away from Emi. "You better go," he said. "Before—"

The rest of his words were lost as suddenly all three of them were drenched in light. Will threw his arm across his eyes. Emi clamped back onto the other one and screamed. There wasn't time to see what Ken did. A harsh voice shouted at them.

"Stop! Don't make a move!" it said.

Before any of them could decide whether to obey or not, rough arms reached into the light and yanked Emi away from Will and snatched him up as if he were a sack of flour. He looked wildly around, just in time to see Ken being tossed over a pair of broad, green-clad shoulders.

It's the army! Will's thoughts told him senselessly. *They don't understand—I'm not a prisoner!*

But they were definitely treating him like one. The guard who handled him did so with all the gentleness of a grizzly bear. Will was almost upside down as the man carried him across the camp, and he only turned him upright again when they had entered the inner room of a building where a naked lightbulb burned from the ceiling. Then he dumped him onto a cot and loomed over him.

"You stay right there, buddy boy," he said. "I have some questions for you—"

And then he stopped and grabbed Will by the front of his

shirt, pulling him up close to his face.

"Hey—you're a white boy!" he said. "What were you doing with these Nips?"

For once in his life, Will couldn't think of a thing to say. It was as if his tongue were glued to the roof of his mouth.

"You were gonna turn them in, weren't you?" the guard said. "Tell me you were gonna turn them in."

Tell him that! Will's brain screamed at him. *Tell him that and he'll let you go!*

But Will's tongue wouldn't come loose, and he was glad because he didn't want to tell him that at all. He shook his head.

"What's the matter with you, boy?" the guard said. He looked completely disgusted as he hissed through his teeth and turned to the other two green-clad guards, who were glaring down at Ken and Emi huddled together on another cot.

"Did you get anything out of them?" Will's guard said.

One of the other guards gave a snort. "Are you kidding? You know they aren't gonna say a word. Look at 'em—they don't even have the decency to look scared. I'd like to slap their blank little faces."

He raised his hand, and Will gasped. But Will's guard put his hand out and pushed the other guard back.

"You're just askin' for trouble," he said. "Besides, I don't know what you expect. They aren't even human, as far as I'm concerned. They never show a feeling—"

Will's tongue chose that moment to come loose. "What do you mean, they're not human? They're humaner than you are! And they weren't doin' anything wrong—in fact, they were trying to get back *into* the camp, and I was helpin' them."

Will's guard was in his face before Will could take another breath.

"Were you now?" he said. "And what were they doing *out* of the camp in the first place?"

Will's mind spun. Now what? He couldn't tell them Emi and Ken were out looking for Yoji. Then there'd be even more trouble. But no lie would come to him. If he was going to say anything at all, he'd better tell at least half the truth.

Summoning all the courage he could scrape up, Will plastered on a smile. "Well," he said, "you know how it is with us kids—when we're shut up for too long, we get restless, you know? So they just slipped out to get a little breathing space—and I found them—and they were lost, but they were trying to find their way back so—I just helped them."

"You lyin' little sack of trash," the guard said. He hissed through his teeth again and let go of Will. "Get their mother in here. I'm sicka lookin' at 'em."

One of the guards left. Will's guard and the other one went to the doorway and talked under their breath. Will himself hardly dared breathe. But he did sneak a look over at Kenichi and Emiko. Emi, of course, was whimpering into her hands. But Ken was looking straight at Will. His eyes were no longer narrowed. His face was no longer tight. Will could read Ken's face just fine. It clearly said, *Thanks for not telling on Yoji.*

It's nothin', Will shrugged back at him. It was a better conversation than any he'd ever had with Herb.

It was only a few minutes before a small Japanese woman appeared in the doorway. Will couldn't take his eyes from her face. Herb had been wrong, he decided. "They" didn't all look alike. This lady was tiny, but she looked as if she could take down all three guards with a single word if she'd wanted to. Right now it was clear all she wanted to do was get her children out of there.

Emi and Ken bolted to her and she folded both of them against her as she looked over their heads at Will's guard. With her dark hair swept back from her face into an arrangement of

bobby-pinned curls, her eyes looked large and smart—and not
at all afraid.

"Have they done something wrong?" she said. Just like her
kids, she sounded American. She also sounded, at least to Will,
as if she had gone to school for a long time.

"They were outside the camp," Will's guard said.

"But they were trying to get back in," Will said.

Ken and Emi's mother looked at Will for the first time. Her
eyebrows went up, but she said nothing.

"You better hold your tongue, youngster," Will's guard said
to him. He turned to the mother. "If it was an escape attempt, it
was a botched one," he said. "Take them back to your apartment,
Mrs. Lin, and whale the tar out of them."

Mrs. Lin nodded, but Will had the feeling she wasn't going
to "whale the tar" out of anyone, unless it was the guard himself. She walked out of the building with the children still clinging to her, but she managed to do it with her head held high
and her shoulders squared. She made Will want to cheer.

Once she was gone, however, the urge to stand up and shout
drained out like the last of the water out of the bathtub. If the
guards had called Emi and Ken's mom, why would they do any
less to him? Will tried not to think about Mom finding out he'd
been arrested.

But the thought he couldn't dismiss was Mom finding out
that he'd been hanging around with "those miserable Japanese."
It wasn't so much how mad she was going to be; it was how he
was going to convince her that Ken and Emi and even Yoji
weren't like that.

He sank back onto the cot. What was going to happen to
them now? The guards hadn't taken Ken and Emi off in chains.
He'd told Mrs. Lin what she should do. But what about Yoji?
Were they going to find out he was still gone? What would they
do if they did? He had a feeling "serious consequences" meant

something completely different here than they did at his house.

"He's in here," Will heard his guard say from the outer room. "You can have him."

Who can have me? Will almost shouted.

But there was no need. The person they ushered into the room was Bud.

Chapter Fifteen

*T*he minute Will spotted Bud, he knew it wasn't going to be long before he started crying. The only thing that stopped him was the thought of the guards seeing him in tears. He bit his lip and held it in.

"Are you all right?" Bud said to him.

Will nodded.

"This the boy you're looking for?" Will's guard said from the doorway.

"This is the one," Bud said. "I'll take him off your hands."

"We don't want to see you around here anymore, son," the guard said to Will. "Taking up with these Japs is not something you want to do—"

"Thanks, officer," Bud said. His voice had an icy sound Will had never heard in it before. "I think I can take it from here."

"Suit yourself," the guard said. Then he shrugged and turned away. Will had the feeling he was forgotten before he even got to Bud's car.

"How did you know I was here?" Will said as they hurried toward it.

"Let's wait until we get out of here," Bud said. "This place gives me the creeps."

Bud wouldn't say a word until they had passed the sign at the front gate, painted nicely on wood with an array of rocks arranged beneath it. Someone had tried to make the Santa Fe Relocation Center look like an inviting place. Will knew differently.

When they were on the road back to town, Bud finally said, "Your mother heard some noise out in the garage. When she got out there, her motorcycle was gone, of course, and she was madder than a wet hen. So she went charging down the driveway to see if she could catch the thief, and what does she find but somebody's journal."

"Yoji's," Will said. "Uh-oh."

"She glanced through it and knew a boy from the camp had been there. From the way he wrote about how important it was to him to take care of his brother and sister and his mother, she suspected he was the kind who would come back with what he'd "borrowed," so she waited on the back steps. She was right. Here came Yoji with the motorcycle."

"What happened?" Will said. "He can be pretty mean-looking."

Bud chuckled. "Not any more so than your mother, evidently. She held him at flashlight-point against the garage, trying to get him to 'fess up."

"Did he?" Will said.

"Nope. She had to keep him there until Fawn finally showed up." Bud chuckled again. "Needless to say, Fawn told the whole story when she got a load of the look on your mom's face. Anyway, that's when Ingrid took the boy—Yoji is his name?"

"Yeah."

"That's when she took him inside and called me."

"I still don't get it," Will said.

"Wait—there's more. I drove all over the east side, which Fawn said was supposed to be your 'beat,' and when I couldn't find you, I decided to bite the bullet and come to the camp. I had no idea how I was going to ask about you or the other two kids, but the guard made it easy for me." Once again, Bud gave his hearty chuckle. "I drove up to the gate and the guard said, 'Have you come for the Anglo kid?' I said, 'Sure,' and then started praying he was talking about you."

"It was me, all right," Will said. "I'm sorry, Bud—I know you're disappointed in me—"

"Why would I be disappointed in you? You were doing a good thing, Will."

Will shook his head. "I bet my mom doesn't think so."

"The only thing your mother doesn't like is that you did all this without asking for her help. But as far as you caring about Yoji and his brother and sister, she's behind you all the way. She's at home right now with Yoji, trying to figure out what she can do to help him. If somebody doesn't, his anger is going to get him into a heap of trouble."

Will knew he was staring so hard his mouth was hanging open, but he couldn't help it. Mom wanted to *help* Yoji? But wasn't he one of the "miserable Japanese"?

"She read enough in his journal to know he's a good kid," Bud was saying. "And I certainly trust your mother's judgment—so I'm going to see what I can do as well." He grinned. "I guess God just wants me to take in strays wherever I find them. It's a tough job, but somebody's got to do it."

Will didn't let himself believe that Mom was all right with what he'd done until he got in the house and saw her pouring oatmeal into a bowl on the table in front of Yoji. He wasn't in handcuffs, and she wasn't holding a baseball bat to his head.

She did give Will a shake after she hugged him, and she did

promise to deal with his "methods" later. But mostly she was worried about Yoji.

Yoji himself barely looked at her, but focused his narrow gaze on Will. "What about Emiko and Kenichi?" he said.

"They're back with your mom," Will said quickly, before Yoji could decide to come out of the chair and do some more shoulder-grabbing. "I helped 'em get back to camp, but we all got caught by the guards." And then he remembered to add: "I didn't tell them that Emi and Ken were out looking for you."

"Thanks," he said gruffly. Then he scraped back his chair and stood up. "I appreciate your help, Mrs. Hutchinson, but I better get back to my family now."

"Oh, I don't think so," Mom said. She put a hand on his shoulder and pushed him gently back into the seat. "I think it would be best if you stayed right here until we can find a way to get your family out, too—"

"No!" Yoji said. His face darkened, and Will shrank back. This was the Yoji he had come to know. "I have to be with my family," he said. "You don't understand."

"Yes, I do," Mom said. "But if you go back, you're sure to be caught, and—"

"I know where to get back in," Yoji said.

"But I hate to see you take a risk when we may be able to bring your family to you here," Mom said.

Yoji's face grew hard. "I can't wait for that," he said. "I have to go to them now. I promised my father I wouldn't leave them."

"All right, how about this," Bud said, one hand on Mom's shoulder and one on Yoji's. "Why don't I drive Yoji back to the spot where he thinks he'll be able to get in without being seen? I can watch, and if it looks like there's going to be trouble, I can take it from there."

"You don't have to," Yoji said.

"Yes, I do, son," Bud said. "I've made promises, too."

"Can I go with you?" Will said.

Mom started to say no—Will could see it coming. But Bud moved his hand from Yoji's shoulder to Will's.

"It's fine with me, Ingrid," he said. "Will has a lot invested in this."

"All right," Mom said in her I-really-don't-want-to-do-this voice. "But at the first sign of trouble, you get down in that backseat and stay there, you understand?"

"Gotcha!" Will said—and then he bolted for the back door before she could change her mind.

"But you're going to have to deal with Fawn when you come back," Mom called after him. "I sent her upstairs to take a bath. She's going to be madder than a hornet when she comes down here and finds out you've gone off without her."

Will did feel bad, but not enough to stay behind. He'd find a way to make it up to her.

Yoji directed Bud to a dirt road that took them almost to the northeast corner of the camp, but he stopped him several hundred yards away.

"I can get closer," Bud said.

"No," Yoji said, pointing to a stand of large junipers inside the barbed wire. "There's two guards hiding in there—I can see them from here."

"Good eye," Bud said. "So now what?"

Yoji stared through the windshield as Bud backed the car up and turned it around. "You could drop me off where my crew's going to be working today," he said. "I could just slip into the group—those guards aren't as sharp as the ones here at the camp. It's a construction site, lots of places to duck in and out of."

"Your crew works on Sunday?" Bud said.

Yoji winced. "No. I didn't realize it was Sunday."

Will hadn't either. The sun was coming up on a new day, breaking through the gray mist of the early morning.

"I always know when it's Sunday," Bud said, chuckling. "I *do* work on the Sabbath!"

Suddenly Yoji snapped his fingers. "That's it," he said. "It's perfect."

"What is?" Will said.

"There's an Episcopal church over on Palace Avenue."

"That would be the Church of the Holy Faith," Bud said. "What about it?"

"They hold a service for people from the camp early on Sunday mornings, before their regular services start—because a lot of people in their congregation don't know about us coming there. If they did, they'd probably leave the church altogether."

Will thought of Herb. He'd said he went to a "boring" church on East Palace Avenue. If this was the one, that made sense. Herb's father would never go to a church where they let "Japs" go—not if he was anything like Herb.

"You could drive me there," Yoji said, "and I could just join my family and melt into the group as they get off the truck. That is, if you don't mind. You've done too much already."

"I haven't done nearly enough, that's plain," Bud said as he headed the rattletrap Chevrolet toward East Palace. "I can see I'm going to have to change this Japanese-having-to-sneak-to-church situation."

All was quiet in front of the Church of the Holy Faith when they drove up. Bud parked the car in the next block and said they'd wait until the truck full of Japanese arrived.

"Too bad you have to ride to church in the back of a truck," Will said.

Yoji grunted. "It isn't as if we're all dressed up in our Sunday best. We don't *have* Sunday best."

"So tell us about yourself while we're waiting," Bud said.

"Not much to tell."

"How about your family? What about your father? You mentioned he's overseas."

"Yeah, that's something, isn't it?" Yoji said. "In 1942 they arrested him because he was Issei and put him here. Then they wanted him to sign the oath, but he didn't—"

"What oath is that?" Bud said.

Yoji's face grew darker. "It's called the Application for Leave Clearance. There are a bunch of questions on it, but there are two in particular that—" Yoji shook his head. "They require a simple yes or no answer. 'Are you willing to serve in the armed forces of the United States, in combat duty, wherever ordered?' and 'Will you swear unqualified allegiance to the United States of America and forswear any form of allegiance or obedience to the Japanese emperor, or any other foreign government?' You had to answer yes to both of those to either serve in the army or be cleared to leave the camps."

"Why couldn't he answer yes?" Will said.

"Because," Yoji said bitterly, "he wasn't allowed to become an American citizen because he was born in Japan—even though he came to the United States when he was five months old. But if he gave up his Japanese citizenship by answering yes, then he wouldn't be a citizen anywhere. So—we stayed in the camp." Yoji gave a laugh that really didn't sound like a laugh at all; there was nothing happy in it. "Then the army sent people to my father practically begging him to come and serve. My father speaks Japanese, and they needed him to work as an interpreter, translating documents they'd captured from the Japanese." Yoji shook his head again. "*I* would never have done it, but for some reason, my father loves this country, in spite of all the things it has done to our family. He gave in and signed the oath, and now he's somewhere in Burma or China."

"He must be with Merrill's Marauders!" Will said. "They're

kicking the Japanese in the tail! I mean, you know—those Japanese . . ."

Yoji shrugged. "Maybe so—but my father going to serve like that also kicked my grandfather in the tail. He was living with us here, and when my father went with the army, he just gave up. He died six months after my father left."

"I'm sorry," Bud said.

"At least he's out of that hole of a camp," Yoji said. "The only reason I'm not is because I promised my father I would take care of my mother and Kenichi and Emiko."

"Speaking of whom," Bud said, "I think that's your family coming now."

There was indeed a truck coming up East Palace with a bed load of Japanese passengers. Yoji nodded at both Will and Bud.

"Thanks," he said. "You've gone out of your way. Don't think I don't appreciate it."

"We'll see you again," Bud said. "Ingrid and I are going to see to it that your whole family gets out of there."

"It's a nice thought," Yoji said, "but I won't hold my breath."

Then he opened the car door and slipped out. As the Japanese people jumped down from the bed of the truck, Yoji blended easily in with them. There was barely a ripple in the crowd, but even from the car Will could see the faces of Ken and Emi and Mrs. Lin. A peace seemed to settle over them. It made Will ache inside.

"What are you thinking, my friend?" Bud said as they pulled away.

"I'm thinking I want to help them," Will said. "Even if Yoji doesn't believe we will."

"You can't blame Yoji for not trusting people, especially us white folks—"

"Hakujin," Will said.

"We'll just have to show him that we're not all like that," Bud said.

"I almost was," Will said. "And I thought Mom was."

"You must have misunderstood your mother," Bud said. "Just ask her about it when we get to your house."

Mom and Fawn were sitting in the living room when Bud dropped Will off and hurried on to get himself ready for Sunday services. Fawn greeted Will with dagger eyes, but Mom wasn't letting that stop what she had to say.

"All right, you two," she said after she'd ordered Will to take his place next to Fawn in the window seat, "for some reason you've both come to the conclusion that I would not want you to help a pair of Japanese children who were in trouble. We can talk later about where you got that idea, but for right now I just want to set you straight: I hate what the Japanese are doing in the Pacific. But I do not hate the Japanese people, especially those living here who have absolutely nothing to do with the horror that is going on over there. Is that understood?"

Will and Fawn both nodded. Will actually wanted to get up and holler, but he figured he was walking on pretty thin ice with Mom as it was. There was no point in pushing it.

"Now, then," Mom went on, "just to make sure there are no further misunderstandings along these lines, there will be no more tearing-down talk in this house, only building-up talk. And that goes for me as much as for the two of you. We have to get back to finding common ground."

Fawn looked at Will. "That goes for you, too, Will Hutchinson," she said.

"What are you looking at me for?"

"You've forgot all about our common ground. You're always leaving me out of things these days."

"No tearing-down talk," Mom said. "Only building-up."

"Then—you better include me—that's all I gotta say."

"I will," Will said. "I want to."

Fawn blinked. "That's it?"

"Yeah, that's it."

"I love it," Mom said. "Now get ready for church, you two. We have a lot of building up to do, and it starts there."

"What do you mean, it starts there?" Fawn said.

"You'll see," Mom said.

They did see. As they sat in their usual row up in the balcony, Bud preached from the pulpit—since Pastor Weston was still away—about the plight of the Japanese-Americans. He said that if the people in the congregation were to be true followers of Jesus, they should do what they could to help the Japanese right there in Santa Fe.

"We cannot hate anything that God has made," he said. "But we must hate those things that men and women do that destroy anything God has made."

Will was sure that as he said it, he looked right up at Will. Just in case he did, Will gave him a thumbs-up sign.

After church, people thronged around Bud, Tina, and Mom outside the front door of the church, asking what they could do to help. Bud was beaming, but Will thought he himself was beaming more. Finally, finally, the tug-of-war was over. He could do what he really wanted to do—he could be friends with Ken and Emi and—

But he didn't even have a chance to finish his thought. The second set of doors burst open, and Montgomery DeWitt stomped out, a cigar already in his mouth.

"What do you think you're doing, Reverend Kates?" he shouted above the din.

A hush fell so hard, Will waited for the ground to shake.

"I'm gathering some disciples," Bud said calmly. "What can I count on you for?"

"I'll tell you what you can count on me for!" Mr. DeWitt cried. "You can count on me to have you removed from the pastorate if you lift a single finger to help a Jap!"

And with that he stalked down the church steps in a flurry of cigar ash.

✝ ✦ ✝

Chapter Sixteen

*W*ill felt like his bicycle tire when the air was escaping from it. Beside him, Abe put his fist in his mouth and gave a low moan. Fawn's fists, on the other hand, were doubled up, and only because Will caught her by the shoulder did she not take off and jump on Mr. DeWitt's departing back.

"Can he do that, Bud?" Tina said. "Can he have you removed?"

"I don't know," Bud said. He chuckled. "I guess we'll find out. Meanwhile, we have work to do."

And work they did, all of them, for the next two weeks.

Bud found out that in other places where there were internment camps—Utah, Wyoming, Colorado, Arizona, Idaho, and Arkansas—there were programs where churches were sponsoring families, helping them make a living outside the camps. Since those people came out of the camps with only what would fit in their suitcases, there was a lot to be done to provide for them. Some of the churches, Bud discovered, had even raised scholarship money so the older kids could go to college.

Bud called a meeting at the church right away to share that

information with the congregation. Just about everyone showed up—including Mr. Montgomery DeWitt. Abe started to whimper the minute he saw him, but Will patted him on the shoulder and told him it would be all right. He wasn't so sure of that himself, though, especially when the minute Bud was finished talking, Mr. DeWitt stood up, already waving his cigar. His eyebrows were going full speed.

"You're a fool, Mr. Kates!" he cried. "You're throwing time and money away, right along with your career!"

"I don't happen to see it that way," Bud said. "I think what I'm doing is exactly what Jesus would have me do."

"Jesus would have you consort with the enemy?" By now there was a bright red spot on each of Mr. DeWitt's cheeks, and the veins were protruding from his forehead. In spite of Will's reassurances, Abe was obviously frightened. He was trying to stuff both fists into his mouth.

"Hey, Abe," Fawn whispered. "Did you ever notice the way the hair sticks out of his nostrils?"

Abe didn't stop whimpering, but he did look.

"Yeah," Will whispered, "and look at his potbelly. It looks like he swallowed a cantaloupe whole."

That at least got rid of one fist and the whimpering. It was going to take more than that to reassure Will himself, though. Mr. DeWitt was preaching to the crowd now, and some of them were nodding their heads.

"Blood is thicker than water, ladies and gentlemen," he was saying, cigar gesturing dramatically. "You don't think the minute those people get out of that camp, they're not going to contact their relatives—the very people who are killing our boys?"

"No, Mr. DeWitt," Mom said. "I don't. And I have a husband over there, being held prisoner."

A woman stood up and said, "She's right!"

Then another person from the back yelled, "I agree!"

A murmur rumbled through the crowd. Most of them stopped nodding at Mr. DeWitt.

"There's no point in trying to talk to you people!" he cried. "It's going to take more than talk to wake you up." He started for the door, then stopped, cigar hanging from the corner of his mouth, wavy gray hair standing up on end. "If anyone sees it my way, follow me. We need to have our own meeting!"

Nobody moved. Mr. DeWitt glared from beneath his eyebrows and stormed out.

"Now then," Bud said with a grin. "Shall we make plans?"

"Yes!" said a man in the back.

"All right, then. Let's start with a prayer."

After they prayed, the plans were laid. If Bud could get approval, the Lin family would stay with the Hutchinsons until their own housing could be found. Others in the church would help Mrs. Lin get a job, maybe as a saleswoman for five dollars a day plus 1 percent commission, or working in a factory.

"She's a lot smarter than that," Will told Fawn.

Several of the women volunteered to see to new clothes, and some of the men started organizing a fund-raiser for college scholarship money for Yoji. Mom assured them that from reading his journal, she knew he was smart.

The plans didn't stop with the First Presbyterian Church, either. Will, of course, told Mr. T. all about it, and his tanned face glowed gold.

"How can I help?" he said. "I'll work on getting Ken—is that his name?—admitted here, and your mother can do the same over at Carlos Gilbert for the little girl. Have her call me tonight."

It was a busy time for the kids, too. Will and Fawn helped Mom divide the attic into separate rooms with some screens they found at a shop in town. She fixed up Mrs. Lin's section, Fawn did Emi's, and Will worked on Ken's. He put a lot of his own stuff in there, and made a separate scrapbook of clippings about Merrill's

Marauders. He still wasn't sure Ken trusted him yet, but he worked at it as if he did. There was, after all, nothing to lose.

On Tuesdays and Thursdays, Abe and Will and sometimes Fawn planned out all kinds of stuff for the kids to do when they arrived. Abe mostly gurgled and nodded and repeated everything Will said, but that was okay. Will had plenty of ideas for both of them.

Finally, on the first of October, Bud called Mom on the phone. He was so excited, Will and Fawn could hear him all the way to the kitchen table.

"They're approved!" he said. "The Lins are going to be set free!"

Fawn let out a whoop that would have split Will's eardrum if he hadn't already been yelling himself. For once, Mom didn't hush them up, and as soon as she hung up the phone, she pulled out a Japanese cookbook she'd found someplace and started deciding what they were going to have the Lins' first night "home."

"Pickled cabbage," she said, "and hot bean paste soup."

Fawn and Will looked at each other. "Maybe we should take them out to LaFonda," Will said.

When Bud pulled up in front of the Hutchinsons' house two days later and ushered the Lins up to the front door, Will was pretty sure they didn't care about food at all. They all looked like they were so nervous they were about to throw up anything they had already eaten. Only Yoji didn't look anxious. He just had a blank look.

"Why are they scared?" Fawn whispered.

"After all they've been through," Mom whispered back, "I don't blame them. We just have to shower them with love, that's all."

That proved to be no problem for Fawn. She grabbed Emi by the hand before she could even get in the door and dragged her, suitcase and all, up the stairs, jabbering the entire way.

Mom held out her hand to Yoji, and he took it, although Will could see he would rather have kept his tucked in his pocket.

"Introduce me to your mother, Yoji," Mom said.

Yoji did, more politely than Will would have expected, and then he said, "Where can I put my stuff?"

"We've given you the guest room," Mom said. "Second floor, first door on your right. We thought you could use the privacy."

Yoji's face got about an inch softer for a moment before it went blank again and he headed for the stairs. Will wondered what his face would do when he found the brand-new journal book Mom had gotten him waiting for him on his bed.

Mom and Mrs. Lin were already arm in arm, strolling toward the kitchen.

"I wanted to make pork and noodles for you," Mom was saying, "but there isn't an ounce of pork to be found. I'm thinking of raising my own pigs—"

They disappeared into the kitchen. That left Will and Ken.

"So, hi," Will said.

"Hi," Ken said. His gaze slanted toward the floor.

"Um, want to see your room?"

Ken shrugged.

"I didn't booby-trap it or anything."

Ken's eyes came up, and his brows came together like a question mark.

"I thought you might think I'd do something like that," Will said. "I mean, after the rocks and everything—"

But he stopped because Ken was shaking his head. "I know I can trust you," he said. "You didn't tell on my brother. Only—"

"Only *what?*" Will said. "Jeepers—what do I have to do, sign it in blood or somethin'?"

"No!" Ken said. "I just wanna know why you're doing all this—why you didn't rat on Yoji and why you want us living here."

" 'Cause I don't hate you," Will said. "And it seems like a lot of other people do. I know what that's like."

"Oh," Ken said.

"So, do you wanna see your room?"

"Sure, I wanna see it." And for the first time, Will saw Ken smile. It crinkled across his face, and it made Will break out in a grin, too.

By the time they all sat down to dinner in the kitchen—where Mom said it was homier than the dining room—most of the anxious looks had disappeared. Yoji was still quiet, but he didn't squash down the lively conversation—and nobody complained about the food. Mom had compromised and put both bean paste soup and pickled cabbage *and* homegrown tomatoes and homemade cornbread on the table. Will had never seen even Abe eat as much as the Lins did. For some reason, that made Mom get all misty-eyed.

They didn't stay to wash the dishes, but all piled into Bud's car again to head for the church for a candlelight service Bud was holding especially for the Lins. The church looked more holy than Will had ever seen it, with the candlelight glowing against the white walls and the hardwood floors gleaming in the warmth.

It would have seemed like heaven itself if the moment Bud stood up to begin the first prayer, Mr. DeWitt hadn't stood up, too, and with him several of the church elders. Mom gave Will an uh-oh look, but she squeezed Mrs. Lin's arm and smiled at her. Will squeezed *Fawn's* arm and held his breath.

"Mr. DeWitt," Bud said, "we are about to hold a prayer service here. I wish you would hold your arguments until after I've—"

"You aren't about to do anything, Mr. Kates," Mr. DeWitt said. The protruding veins were absent tonight. He actually looked rather pleased with himself, as far as Will could tell. "The elders here have a petition for you, signed by several members of the congregation, stating that if you continue to aid the enemy, you will be asked to leave the church." He waved his hand toward the document one of the men was unfolding. Will was surprised he wasn't holding a cigar.

Bud glanced at the paper. "There aren't enough signatures on here to make this valid," he said.

"There will be more, trust me," Mr. DeWitt said. "I've only just begun."

Bud looked at him for a long moment. It struck Will that he didn't look at all like Elmer Fudd just then. He looked so strong, in fact, that Abe wasn't even whimpering or chewing on his fist.

"Mr. DeWitt," Bud said finally, "do what you feel you have to do. But in the meantime, I'm going to do what I have to do. Now, if you'll excuse us, we have some praying to do."

Mr. DeWitt shook his gray head and smiled importantly. "I think you'll regret this," he said. "You—and anyone here who assists you—could wind up in a great deal of trouble. I intend to take this all the way to the courts if necessary, and if I win, there could be legal consequences for all of you."

And then he strode down the aisle, leading the elders as if they were his train of servants. Will was about to whisper a comment about the cantaloupe belly peeking out from under his pinstriped vest when two people sitting in front of them stood up and shuffled out into the aisle.

"Where are they going?" Fawn hissed.

Apparently they were following Mr. DeWitt. So were several people on the other side of the church. Will glanced at Ken, and he wished he hadn't. He was staring into his lap, and his face was slowly going blank, just like Yoji's.

"They're just a bunch of cowards," Will whispered to him. "Don't worry about them."

Bud went on with the service, and those who were left prayed and sang loud and strong.

"I hope you're reassured by God's presence," Bud said to the

Lins when the service was over and the candles were being put out.

Mrs. Lin shook her head. "I've always known God is there for us, Reverend Kates," she said, "but I don't expect you to be. Don't make this sacrifice for us. You've made a beautiful gesture, all of you, and we're uplifted by it, but we'll go back to the camp—"

"Mrs. Lin," Bud said. He smothered both her hands with his pudgy ones. "If I wanted to lead my congregation in making a beautiful gesture, we'd put in stained-glass windows. But that's not what we're about here. We're about loving what *God* has made." He swept his now-misty eyes over the kids. There was a lot of tears-in-the-eyes going on tonight, Will decided.

"God has certainly made these kids of yours," Bud said. "Why let them waste their childhoods away because some people hate? We can't do that here."

Will nudged Ken and whispered, "See? It's gonna be okay."

He was completely sure of that the next morning when he and Ken climbed the steps to the open jaws of Harrington Junior High. Ken was wearing clothes newer than the ones Will had on, and he was carrying a brand-new book bag and looking smart and even a little bit tough. Will felt his own chest puffing out some, just to be walking with him.

That lasted about five minutes—just long enough for them to walk down the hall and run into Herb and Glasses Boy and the two boys with the scars on their foreheads. Herb shoved right through them with both hands and blocked Will and Ken's way with his hulk of a body.

"What's *he* doing here?" he said, jerking his red head in Ken's direction.

"He goes to school here now," Will said.

"A *Jap?* You gotta be kiddin'!"

"No, I'm not kiddin'," Will said, "and he's not a Jap. He's a Japanese-American."

"This ain't no American! He's a Nip. He's stinkin' yellow vermin!"

"You forgot viper," Will said. He grinned at Ken. Slowly, Ken grinned back.

"You're smilin' now, Slant-Eyes," Herb said. "But you won't be for long."

"What are you gonna do, Herb?" Will said. "Slug him right here in the hall?"

There was a crowd around them by now, and a few of the boys yelled, "Fight! Let's see a fight!" Herb ignored them.

"No," he said. "I ain't stupid. But you just watch your back, Slant-Eyes." He glanced over his shoulder at his friends, and for the first time Will looked at them, too. It took them a telltale five seconds before they nodded their heads.

"There's a whole gang of them," Ken whispered after he and Will had elbowed their way through the crowd toward class.

"Yeah, but they're not as loyal to Herb as he thinks they are," Will said. "Don't worry about it. I'm not gonna leave your side."

Will was true to his word, and he even took Ken to the office with him during lunch. Mr. T. invited Ken to come in and sit on a saddle chair and tell him about himself while Will ran his errands. Will was actually whistling as he walked down the hall after taking a note to one of the teachers. Both his whistling and his footsteps stopped when he saw the front doors open and two sheriff's deputies step in.

They were walking tall and stiff and not looking to either side. Somehow, Will already knew they were heading for the office. He followed them.

"Mr. Tarantino in?" one of them said to the secretary.

"He's with a student," she said.

"Well, now he's with us," the deputy said.

The other one opened the door to Mr. T.'s office and then looked back at his partner with a half-grin on his face. "Looks like we'll be able to kill two birds with one stone," he said. He turned back to the office doorway where Mr. T. was now standing, his face somber.

"What can I do for you?" Mr. T. said.

"Mr. Tarantino," the deputy said, "we have orders to escort you and young Mr. Lin here off the school grounds. Looks like the school board doesn't want either one of you here."

Chapter Seventeen

*W*ill shoved past a deputy and tried to get past the second one—who grabbed him by the arm and pushed him back.

"Will, it's all right," Mr. T. said.

"No, it's not! You want me to call somebody?" Behind him, Will heard the secretary pick up the phone.

"Who would you call, kid?" the deputy said. "We've got the school board, the sheriff, and a judge making this decision."

"Try FDR," the other deputy said dryly. "Mr. Tarantino, if you will?"

Mr. T. reached back into his office and put his arm around Ken. The boy's face was a blank, except for his eyes. They were beginning to spark anger.

"Don't worry, Ken!" Will said. "I'll get this straightened out—"

"Who is this kid, anyway?" said the deputy who was opening the door into the hallway. "Does he think he's some big shot?"

"Will, you go on to class now," Mr. T. said. Then he followed the deputy out the door. But as they passed through, Will heard

Mr. T. say, "Don't underestimate the boy. He gets things done."

It was this last comment which directed Will's feet, not down the hall to class but out the front door behind the two deputies and Mr. T. and Ken. By the time they went, blinking, out into the October sunlight, there was a crowd of students on either side of the front steps. The word had obviously gotten around somehow.

"Hey, Hutchinson!" a familiar voice yelled. "I *told* your boy to watch his back!"

Will didn't even look at Herb. He kept his eyes directly on Ken and prayed. *God, please don't let him explode or try to run away. Please—make him wait until we can do something—something right.*

Whether Ken felt it or not, Will couldn't tell. He did cooperate as the deputies put him in the car, amid some hisses from the crowd.

But when the officer took Mr. Tarantino's arm, a roar went up that was probably heard all the way to the LaFonda Hotel.

"Hey, where you takin' Mr. T.?"

"He ain't done nothin' wrong!"

"Why you takin' him to jail?"

The deputies acted as if they didn't hear a word. They simply guided Mr. T. into the backseat, climbed into the front, and drove away. A pack of kids started to run after the car, but teachers quickly herded them back and barked for everyone to return to class. Will turned and trudged, unseeing, through the front doors.

"Hey, are you Hutchinson?" somebody said.

Will turned to a Hispanic boy, one he'd seen in Mr. T.'s office before, and nodded.

"What did that Anglo mean about the Japanese kid being 'your boy'?"

"My family helped get him out of the camp," Will said.

He turned again to move on, but the Hispanic kid grabbed his arm. "Why you gotta make trouble for Mr. T.?" he said.

"Yeah," said another kid. "We like him here. Why you gotta get him throwed out?"

"I didn't get him thrown out!" Will said. "Talk to the stupid school board!"

"Whatta they got to do with it?" a kid said.

But the first boy waved him off and got his face close to Will's. "Whatchoo mean?" he said. "What's goin' on?"

Will wanted to run, to go talk to somebody who would even care—somebody who could do something. But it came to him like a brick falling on his head: *Without Mr. T., there* isn't *anybody here that understands. And these kids know it, too.*

Will focused his eyes on the Hispanic kid. He really looked like he was waiting for an answer. "All right," Will said. "I'll tell you what's goin' on."

He told them about the internment camp, about how awful it was and how kids like Ken had had to give up everything for no reason. He told them how Mr. T. felt about them, and how happy he'd been to be able to do something for Ken and maybe someday soon for other kids, too. By the time he got to the part about the deputies being smart alecks in the office, a bigger crowd had gathered around him, and it was an angry one.

"They got no right doin' that to Mr. T.!" the first Hispanic boy said.

The mob agreed, at the tops of their voices.

And then an adult voice shouted over them: "What's going on here?"

Some of the kids scattered. Some of them didn't. The assistant principal, a man Will didn't know very well, swatted them away like they were a bunch of annoying flies and turned to Will.

"Are you responsible for this little gathering?" he said.

"I was just telling them—"

"Well, don't," the man said. "Now go on, get to class. Who's your teacher?"

"That would be me, Mr. Fuches." It was Mrs. Rodriguez. To Will's surprise, she put her arm around his shoulders and smiled a square smile at the assistant principal. "I'll take him."

"Talk some sense into him," Mr. Fuches muttered into his big black moustache. And then he turned on his heel and went the other way.

"I wasn't trying to make trouble," Will said.

"I know," Mrs. Rodriguez said. She gave Will's shoulders a squeeze before she let go. "Matter of fact, it sounded like you were talking perfect sense. Now, where are you going to go from here?"

"To class," Will said.

"No, I mean what are you going to do about this thing now? You've given them the facts. They're all steamed up. Are you just going to let that fester, or are you going to do something about it?"

Will was staring at the side of her square face. "Like what?" he said.

"Haven't you been listening in class, Will Hutchinson?" she said. She cocked her head so that she was looking at him through a panel of her long hair. He wasn't sure, but he thought she was smiling.

"I always listen," Will said.

"Then think about labor unions," she said. "Think about them hard."

She opened the classroom door and ushered him in. When he sat down at his desk, Herb made the kissing sound behind him. Then he hissed. Then he poked Will sharply in the back. Will ignored it all. He was too busy looking up labor unions in his textbook.

There they were—with their picket lines and their sit-down strikes.

Huh, Will thought. *Just call me John L. Lewis.*

All he could think about the rest of the day were strikes. Even

when he and Abe were playing checkers and waiting for the phone
to ring with news of Mr. T. and Ken, even while he was envisioning
Ken behind bars, worse off than he was in the camp, his mind
kept flipping back to lines of men carrying protest signs.

He was still thinking about it when Tina came home and Will
headed for his house on foot. That was probably why he didn't see
Herb and his friends until they were already on him, and then it
was too late to dodge the barrage of eggs they pelted at him.
Within 15 seconds, he was covered in yolks and shells and listening to their fading jeers and footsteps as they took off down the
Paseo de Peralta.

They told me to watch my back, he said to himself. *They
weren't kiddin'.*

And then, without really understanding why at first, he started
to laugh. "Eggshells?" he said out loud. "They think eggshells are
gonna stop me? They're hakujin! Crazy hakujin!"

He was still guffawing when he got to his back door. Mom
didn't see the humor. She just broke out the garden hose and
doused him with water cold enough to freeze his eyebrows while
Mrs. Lin finished cooking supper. Yoji stood on the back porch, an
"I told you so" look on his face.

"So what happened with Ken and Mr. T.?" Will sputtered as
Mom hosed him down.

"Ken's here now. Mr. Tarantino has been told by the school
board that he is not allowed back in the school building unless he
refuses admittance to Ken. It's no surprise, really. I didn't realize
until today that Montgomery DeWitt is on the school board."

"Oh, yeah," Will said. "Mr. T. told me that a long time ago. So
what's Mr. T. gonna do?"

"He's certainly not going to keep Ken out of school, so there
you are."

Will yanked his head out from under the water. He was no

longer laughing. "What do you mean, 'there you are'? They can't fire him, can they?"

"If he refuses to work their way, yes, they can." Mom paused for a moment. "I'm going to need to do something."

"What does *that* mean?" Will said.

"Supper's ready," Mrs. Lin called just then from the porch.

"It smells wonderful," Mom said. "I think you and I ought to open a restaurant together, Tora."

"What does that *mean*, Mom?" Will asked again.

"Fawn! Throw a towel out here for Will, would you?"

Mom's mouth twitched as she put a hand on Will's shoulder. "It means they wouldn't let me bring Emiko into my school building, so I walked out. I'm going to teach Emi and Ken at home until this is resolved, but it's going to be tight money-wise. No movies for a while until I find another job."

She caught the towel Fawn flung from the porch and handed it to Will. "Get dried off. You don't want to miss supper."

Everybody at the table was in a surprisingly good mood, thanks to Mom, Will decided. Ken told them all about what it was like at the sheriff's office where he'd had to wait until Bud could pick him up. The anger was gone from his eyes, which Will knew was probably thanks to Bud. But it was very clearly there in Yoji's.

Still, the air stayed light and they were all oohing over Mrs. Lin's custard when there was a tap on the back door and Bud came in. One look at his face and Will knew *he* wasn't in a good mood. The usually beaming cheeks were sagging and sallow.

"This is a happy group," Bud said.

He tried to smile, but Mom shook her head. "Don't try covering up, Bud. You look awful. What's going on?"

Bud bunched up his lips and looked at the wall. "I've been asked to take a leave of absence until Reverend Weston returns."

"That ridiculous petition?" Mom said. "Did Montgomery DeWitt actually get enough signatures—"

"No," Bud said. "It was the elders. They don't like the division this is causing in the church and they're asking me to step aside for a while, just until the senior pastor comes back. They've invited a retired pastor from Albuquerque to fill in."

"We don't want some old guy!" Fawn said. "We want you!"

Bud smiled faintly and patted her shoulder.

"That means no pay for you, doesn't it?" Mom said.

"Right—but Tina's working—"

"And barely making enough to holler at." Mom pressed her lips together for a second. Then she said, "We will talk about this, Bud. I mean it. I have Aunt Gussie's inheritance—"

"There's no need to talk," Mrs. Lin said. She looked tall in the chair. "I think the children and I should just go back to the camp. We've caused you all so much trouble—"

"No." Bud's voice was so firm, they all looked at him, even Yoji.

"No," he said, "what we have to do is we have to pray. Right here. Right now. Come on—everyone, join hands."

Fawn and Emi made room for him in the circle at the table, and palms fumbled for palms all around. Will held Ken's hand on one side, Fawn's on the other. As Bud began to pray, and Mom chimed in, and Mrs. Lin softly added her own words, Will couldn't stop looking at the hands.

White hands were clasped to golden ones and golden ones to brown. It was men and women, kids and grown-ups, angry people and peaceful ones. They were all different, and yet hooked together the way they were right now, they could have been one big person. One big, strong person.

Dad would paint this if he saw it, Will thought suddenly. *I bet Dad even does this. I bet he makes the other prisoners hold hands and pray every day, just like this.*

The voices went on around him. Even Fawn and Emi and Ken

were joining in now. Will could only hold onto one thought: Dad *was* strong like they were if he was doing this. He was going to make it. And so were they.

Chapter Eighteen

F awn came into his room that night when he was making his signs. She didn't appear to notice them at first. She was too busy bubbling over.

"Emi coming here is the best thing that ever happened," she said. "Except for Mama Hutchie letting *me* come here, of course. She's the best, Emi is. We played out in the back the whole time after I got home from school. She can climb trees even higher than I can, and we wanna challenge you and Ken to a race. I bet we beat—hey, what are you doing?"

Will rocked back from the plank of wood on the floor and put the paintbrush on top of the can.

"Getting ready for the picket line," he said.

"If Mr. T. and the Japanese can't come here," she read, "neither will we." She blinked at Will. "I don't get it."

"That's because you haven't learned about labor strikes yet."

"So are you gonna tell me, or do I have to wrestle it out of you?"

Will pulled out another piece of plank he'd found in the garage and started on a second sign. "It's simple," he said. "When labor doesn't think something's fair, they go on strike—which means they don't work—until somebody does something to make it fair. And while they're striking, they tell everybody how unfair the thing is by carrying signs up and down in front of the factory."

"What factory?" Fawn said.

"No factory in our case. For us, it's the school."

Fawn's eyes grew round. "You mean, you're not gonna go to school until they let Mr. T. and Ken back in?"

"Yep. And I'm gonna advertise."

"You're gonna carry *two* signs?"

"Nope. I'm hoping I'll get some help."

Fawn folded her arms in a huff. "I wanna help. It's no fair I have to go to stupid old St. Catherine's. It'd be so much better if Emi was there, too—"

Her voice drifted off and her eyes clicked with Will's. "I just had the best idea!" she said.

"So go talk to Mom," Will said.

She bolted for the door, and then stopped and said, "Good luck tomorrow. I'll be praying for you."

I hope so, Will thought, *'cause I'm gonna need it*.

The next day, Will hauled his signs to school on the bus, covered in one of Mom's old sheets. She didn't ask any questions when she saw them. She just said, "Use them to build up, not to tear down."

Will repeated that to himself all the way to school. It made it easier to hold up the sign when he got there and walk up and down in front of the steps, even when the first few kids who passed him stopped and stared and said, "What are you, nuts?"

"Nope," Will said. "I'm just strikin'."

"Seventh graders," some kids said.

"Jap-lover," others said.

But that wasn't all of them. There were plenty of kids who

stopped, asked questions, and looked as if they'd halfway like to pick up the other sign and join him. But nobody did.

Not until about 10 minutes before the last bell was supposed to ring. The Hispanic boy Will had talked to the day before, the one he'd seen in Mr. T.'s office sometimes, stood right in front of him and read the sign out loud.

"You mean that?" he said.

"Yeah," Will said.

"Can anybody do it?"

"Sure," Will said. "I got another sign."

"Then lemme have it."

The boy, whose name turned out to be Juan-Carlos, grabbed the other sign and held it high over his head. "You just walk up and down?" he said.

"Yep," Will said.

"Huh," Juan-Carlos said. And he fell into step behind Will.

Seconds later, the front steps were peppered with Juan-Carlos's friends, all wanting to know what he was doing. When he explained, they wanted to join in.

"I don't have any more signs," Will said.

"You got paper," Juan-Carlos said to them. "Make your own."

Some of the things they scratched out on paper with stubs of pencils were barely readable, but Will didn't care. The more kids who joined them, the stronger he felt, and it seemed that the stronger he felt, the more kids wanted to join them.

By the time the final bell rang, the sidewalk was crammed with protesters, quietly marching up and down with their signs. The rest of the students all seemed to be hanging out the windows above them, calling down questions. Very few of them were jeering anymore. Except for four latecomers who straggled down the sidewalk.

"What do you think you're doin', Hutchinson?" Herb Vickers said.

"Nothing you'd understand," Will said.

"I know what he's doing," said Glasses Boy, squinting both eyes at Will's sign. "He's staying out of class until his demands are met."

"Out of class?" said one of the other boys. "Hey, that's for me!"

He and the other Anglo-Hispanic started to open their book bags, but Will shook his head at them. "We don't want you out here just because you don't wanna go to class," he said. "You can only do this if you believe in it."

"Then you can forget it," Herb said. "We aren't goin' to school with no Japs."

"Any 'Japs,' " said a correcting voice behind them. "And we've been through this before: it's Japanese, not Japs."

Will stared. It was Mrs. Rodriguez, and she wasn't scowling. In fact, she even gave a square smile as she said to Herb, "You and your little banditos need to get inside."

"Them too?" Herb said, pointing at Will and his fellow strikers.

"Oh, no, they can stay out here. Matter of fact, I think I'll join them."

Then she directed her square smile at Will and pulled a sign out of her jacket. 'I won't teach in an unfair school,' it said.

"It was the best I could do on a moment's notice," she said to Will as she hoisted it over her head. "You should have given me more warning. Of course, with you, I should have known what you'd be up to as soon as I put the idea in your head." Then she smiled again and fell in with the rest of the marchers.

It wasn't long before two other teachers and several more students joined them with signs. And it wasn't long after that before Mr. Fuches came running down the front steps, moustache standing up like hackles.

"Here comes your first obstacle, Will," Mrs. Rodriguez said. "Stand your ground and I'll stand behind you."

Will planted his feet on the sidewalk. Out of the corner of his eye, he could see the other kids and teachers doing the same.

"All right, enough of this nonsense!" Mr. Fuches called out as he bustled toward them. "Come on, all of you—inside."

He stood impatiently tapping his foot, as if he were trying to corral a flock of ducks. Will didn't move, and neither did anyone else. The moustache stood up again.

"Mrs. Rodriguez—all you teachers. Don't you know your jobs are in jeopardy for this kind of thing?"

"Actually not, Mr. Fuches," Mrs. Rodriguez said. "We have a right to engage in peaceful demonstration. I can give you the article number if you'd like—"

Mr. Fuches batted his hand in her direction and turned to Will. "You!" he said. "I thought I told *you* not to stir things up."

Will looked at Mrs. Rodriguez. She gave him a little nod.

"I haven't stirred anything up," he said. "I was just walking up and down with a sign, and these people joined me."

"Well, perhaps if you just walk yourself back into the school building, they'll join you in *that*, too." The sarcasm seemed to be dripping right off of his moustache. Mom, Will decided, would have called that tearing-down talk.

"That wouldn't build anybody up, Mr. Fuches," Will said. "And that's what I'm trying to do. The school board's tearing down— I'm building up. We all are."

The rest of the picket line nodded.

"Oh, for heaven's sake, kid," Mr. Fuches said. "Knock it off and get your tail back in that building—now!"

He reached out and made a grab for Will's arm. Will stepped back, and Mrs. Rodriguez helped him with a grab of her own.

"Stand your ground, Will," she whispered.

With her holding onto his arm, Will knew just what she meant. He dropped his sign and snatched up Juan-Carlos's hand.

"Grab his hand!" he said to Juan, jerking his head toward the next kid in the line.

Juan-Carlos seemed to understand right away. He took the hand of the boy next to him. All up and down the sidewalk, picketing teachers and kids let go of their signs and held on to each other. It was an instant wall in front of Mr. Fuches.

"Mr. T. would be proud of you," Mrs. Rodriguez whispered to him.

"Mr. F. sure isn't," Will whispered back.

"Mr. F." was at that moment turning purple as he shouted to his secretary who was watching from the front steps: "Call the police!"

Will felt a shiver go up his spine. If anybody else in the line felt it, they didn't show it. They just held hands tighter and waited.

The sheriff's deputies must have been close by, because within minutes sirens were screaming down the block. By then, Will was sure every person in the school was either leaning out a window or standing on the front lawn. If any learning was going to happen at Harrington Junior High that morning, it was going to happen out there on the street.

Will was relieved to see that the two deputies who climbed out of the car were not the same ones who had taken Mr. T. and Ken away the day before. These two looked much more amused than anything else as they hooked their thumbs into their gun belts and surveyed the picket line.

"So this is your riot?" one of them said. He was tall and broad-shouldered and he dwarfed Mr. Fuches.

"Yes!" said Mr. Fuches. "I want all of them arrested."

"Oh, come on," the other deputy said. He looked at the line over the top of his sunglasses. "We're not going to haul in 50 12-year-olds because they don't want to go to school. This is your problem, sir."

Will cleared his throat. "Um, excuse me," he said. "We're not out here because we don't want to go to school. We're protesting

Mr. Tarantino's removal because he admitted a Japanese student."

"Ah," Broad Shoulders said. "I heard about that. Mr. T.'s a good man. Can't say I blame you."

"What?" Mr. Fuches looked like he was about to explode.

"Look, this is a peaceful demonstration," Sunglasses said.

"But—but they're all truant! If they want to demonstrate after school, that's one thing. But the law says they have to be in school!"

"Unless their parents give them permission," Mrs. Rodriguez said.

"What are you doing?" Will whispered. "These kids don't all have permission!"

"I think that can be easily arranged," she said. She nodded down the block and Will looked. There was a train of vehicles pulling up to the curb, led by a motorcycle and a dilapidated Chevrolet. When Mom and Mrs. Lin climbed off the motorcycle, Will almost laughed. He would have, except he was too busy staring at the adults who were getting out of their own cars and marching down the street behind Mom and Mrs. Lin and Bud and Tina—and even Yoji—like they were on some kind of mission.

"That's my mother," Juan-Carlos whispered. "I think I'm in big trouble."

"I don't think so," Mrs. Rodriguez said. "Just trust me."

There wasn't time to find out what she was talking about. The parents had arrived at the sidewalk, and Mom was stepping up to Shoulders.

"If you're here to arrest our children," she said, "don't waste your time. We've come to give them our permission to stage this strike."

"We're not stopping there," said a Hispanic woman behind her. "We're going to join them!"

Juan-Carlos gave Will a jab. "That's my mother, all right!"

Will didn't bother to remind him that two minutes before he'd thought she was going to snatch him out of the line by his hair. He just let go of his hand so he could grab onto Mom's. The line now stretched all the way down the block. Mr. Fuches was purple. He screamed at his secretary this time: "Call DeWitt!"

"Don't bother," Mom said. "He's already on his way."

"How do you know?" Will said.

"Because the man is everywhere," she said. "Besides—I called him."

Will stared. "Why'd you do that, Mom?"

"Because it's time this came to a head. How are you doing, Yoji?"

Will looked at Yoji, really looked at him, for the first time. He was on the other side of Mom, holding hands with her and Juan-Carlos's mother. His face was still blank, but there was no fire in his eyes. There was only caution.

Please, God, Will prayed. *Let Mom be right about this. Don't let this tear Yoji down any more.*

Mom was right about one thing—Montgomery DeWitt was on his way, and he arrived just as Shoulders and Sunglasses were about to leave. Will guessed that it was the way he slammed his car door—and the way the mob behind him slammed theirs—that kept the two deputies there. Will felt his hands go clammy inside Mom's and Mrs. Rodriguez's.

"Look at that," Mom said. "Every one of them is gnawing on a cigar."

"Except the women," Mrs. Rodriguez said.

Mom's mouth twitched. "Remind me to have you over for dinner as soon as this whole mess is over."

That couldn't happen soon enough for Will, although he was certain he would never eat again. His stomach was in a huge knot.

"Now what is he doing here?" Mom said.

"Who?" Will said. "Is it FDR?"

"Who—no, it's that strange man that's always hanging around LaFonda."

"Looks like he's hanging around here now," Mrs. Rodriguez said.

The man did look as if he were just there to watch. He stood apart from Mr. DeWitt's mob, which was lining up across from Will's group, and leaned against a light pole. As always, his eyebrows moved up and down together over his steel-rimmed glasses for no apparent reason as he smoked his pipe.

But Will couldn't focus on him. Mr. DeWitt was stirring his people up, and their shouts drowned out everything else.

"Jap-lovers—you're Jap-lovers, all of you!"

"You're killing our boys overseas!"

"You're as bad as the Nips!"

"You oughta be locked up, too!"

"Stop this—stop this now!"

That last shout came from Bud. How he managed to shut them all up, Will didn't know. He had a feeling most of the people with Mr. DeWitt were already tired of shouting. They looked almost relieved when Bud strode out in front of them.

"Go, Bud," Mom whispered. "God be with you."

"Let's stop this now, people," Bud said. "I'm surprised at all of you, shouting hateful things out here in front of these children. We're not here about hate. We're about—"

"Don't give us that love nonsense again, Kates," Mr. DeWitt shouted. His voice sounded shrill, like the barking of some small, yappy dog. "These kids don't know *what* they're about. You've just put some un-American ideas in their heads and gotten them all stirred up and they're seeing it as an excuse to get out of school. If Tarantino had been any kind of principal in the first place, this wouldn't be happening."

"Mr. Tarantino has taught these children to know injustice when they see it," Bud said. His voice, now completely un-Fudd-like, sounded strong and sure. "They're good kids."

"Good? They're going to grow up and ruin this country if we allow this to go on! You show me one good kid in that whole lot."

"I'd bet my life they're all good," Bud said. "But I'll show you one. Will—tell the man."

Will swallowed. There had been nothing in the textbook about guys having to step out of the picket line and give speeches. He looked wildly at Mrs. Rodriguez.

"Don't give me that look," she said, smiling squarely. "You do this all the time in my class. Let him have it."

"Go, Will," Mom whispered. "Build 'em up."

Will dropped Mom's hand and Mrs. Rodriguez's and rubbed his own together. They were oozing sweat, and he wasn't sure his mouth would open. It did, somehow, and words actually came out.

"My dad," he said, "is overseas in a prisoner-of-war camp. A lot of us got dads over there, fightin' and stuff. Even Yoji's dad is there—in the American Army—right in the middle of China." He swallowed again and looked at Mom. She was nodding. And so was Yoji. "They're fightin' to build things back up," Will went on. "We can't be over here, tearin' things down. And that's what you're doin', Mr. DeWitt. You're tearin' people down, and that's wrong. We can hate the stuff that people do, but we can't hate the people. We gotta—we gotta love 'em. We gotta treat 'em fair. We gotta make up for it when we do the wrong thing to 'em. That's why we got the Lins out of the camp and that's why we're helpin' 'em—so we can build back up what got taken away."

There was a long pause—and then the crowd started to cheer. Mr. DeWitt cut them off with a wild wave of his cigar.

"It's talk—nothing but talk he's heard from his preacher!" Mr. DeWitt cried. "And a preacher who's been drummed out of the church—"

"Stick to the subject, Mr. DeWitt," said Juan-Carlos's mother.

"This *is* the subject. This boy can talk all he wants about building up, but as long as Japs are Japs and Americans are Americans, there's gonna be trouble. You can't put 'em together. I'm tellin' you, we can't put 'em together—"

The crowd began to buzz just then. It took Will a moment to see why.

Yoji had let go of the hands on either side of him, and he was moving toward Will. He stopped in front of him and nodded his head for Will to step forward. Will didn't have to look at Mom or Mrs. Rodriguez. He went right up to Yoji, and he put out his hand. Yoji didn't wait, either. He put his hand in Will's and he shook it, and he gripped Will's shoulder with his other hand.

"You're a friend," he said to Will. Then he looked up at Mr. DeWitt and he said, "This is my friend. I trust him with my life."

It was apparently more than Mr. DeWitt could take. He thrust his beloved cigar aside and made a lunge for Yoji. Shoulders and Sunglasses had him on both sides before he ever got there.

The crowd began a dull roar, but this time it was another voice that stopped them. "Agent Graves," it said. "FBI. I'd like to say a few words if you'll allow me."

The crowd turned almost as one person to look at the bored man with the pipe, leaning against the light pole. He moved his eyebrows up and down and stepped out between the two lines, Mr. DeWitt's and Will's.

"FBI?" Will murmured. "Wait'll Fawn hears this."

"Check his credentials!" Mr. DeWitt barked at the deputies.

They ignored him, but Agent Graves flipped out a wallet and flashed it before them.

"He's a fraud!" DeWitt shouted. "Or he would have spoken up by now."

"Would you just shut up?" Sunglasses said.

"I haven't said anything during this entire fiasco," Agent Graves said in the bored voice Will would have expected out of him, "because this is not my business here in Santa Fe. But I think I can be of some assistance to you in giving you some information you aren't yet privy to."

Will didn't understand half the words he was using, but he got the idea that this man was on their side.

"There are new documents being signed by the president every day," Agent Graves said. "One of the latest states that if a family of Japanese origin is legally released from a relocation camp and has visible means of support, its members can by law remain in the community, and by law the public school system is obliged to admit school-age students to its schools."

"We'll have that law changed!" Mr. DeWitt cried.

"You certainly have the right to take it to court," Agent Graves said, his voice in the same monotone he'd been using all along. "By the time any resolution is reached, of course, the war will probably be over."

"Then we'll run them out of town!"

"And then the National Guard will be brought in, but why waste money for the war effort on that? Besides—" Agent Graves stopped, took a puff on his pipe, and then motioned it toward Will. "I wouldn't advise standing up to this boy and his group anyway. I don't see how you'd win."

With that he replaced the pipe in his mouth and, stuffing his hands into his pockets, wandered off down the street as if he had merely gotten tired of the scene. Behind him, the crowd went wild with cheering.

"Mrs. Hutchinson," Shoulders said to Mom, "I think it would be wise to take your family home. They've made their point."

"I understand," she said. "Who wants to ride with me on the motorcycle?"

"Me," Will said. After all, it would be a good excuse to hold onto Mom without looking like a sissy. Right now, that was all he wanted to do.

In the next few weeks, October turned into November, bringing with it more changes than gold leaves on the aspen trees and frost on the windows.

The people at First Presbyterian raised enough money for Yoji to start college in January. Yoji spent less time off by himself writing in his journal and more time working on the house they found for the Lins to rent. It needed a few repairs, but Yoji had the construction experience. A few times Will went to help. He never saw the anger in Yoji's eyes again.

Reverend Weston came back to town and immediately allowed Bud to return to his job at the church. Rumor had it that he also gave the elders a stern lecture about love.

As soon as Bud was back in, three more families from the camp were sponsored and set free. Fawn was a little afraid Emi would want to play with those girls more than with her, but Emi assured Fawn that she was the only girl she knew who was just like her.

"And I'd hoped there was only one of you, Fawn," Mom said with a twitch of her lips.

Bud also arranged it so that the families who were still in the camp could worship at First Presbyterian on Sundays with everyone else. After that, Mr. DeWitt started going to the Episcopal church. Will didn't know what he'd do if he found out the Japanese were secretly worshiping there, too.

Mom went back to work at Carlos Gilbert, but Emi didn't go with her. Mom used some of the money she'd inherited from Aunt Gussie to send her to St. Catherine's with Fawn.

Mr. Tarantino went back to work too, and both he and Mrs. Rodriguez came over for dinner one night. That's when Will found out that Mrs. Rodriguez's husband was off at war too, and that's when he discovered how it was that all the parents had shown up on protest day, just at the right time.

"When I saw you out there, Will," Mrs. Rodriguez said, "my heart just went out to you. Now, you're a tough little rascal, but I knew you were going to need a lot of help—so I got Mrs. Torres and Mr. Marin to start calling parents while I made my sign and got on down there."

"Sounds like everybody got along fine without me," Mr. T. said. "Maybe I'll just take a vacation."

"Please don't," Mom said. "I'm afraid Will would try to take over the whole place—and I need him for chores."

Bigger things were happening, too. Franklin Roosevelt was re-elected President. There was still talk that the war might be over by Christmas, although the Allies had declared it would have to be an unconditional surrender by Germany, Italy, and Japan before they would officially end it. Mrs. Rodriguez explained to the class that that meant the future of those countries would be decided by the Allies, and none of them was ready for that yet. Besides, there was talk that Germany was developing a "wonder weapon" and that the U.S. was coming up with one, too. Some people even said that had something to do with why Agent Graves was in town. Will couldn't see what that had to do with it.

Meanwhile, the Hutchinsons, the Kateses, and the Lins declared their own small victory and prepared for the biggest Thanksgiving everybody could afford. Will was definitely thankful, especially when Herb Vickers made it a point the day before to tell him that his father said he was never to speak to Will again.

"You're speaking to me now, aren't you?" Will said, grinning at Ken.

"You just watch your back!" Herb said.

Will didn't lose any sleep over that. After all, Glasses Boy and the other two kids had stopped hanging around with Herb. In fact, Glasses Boy—Neddie—turned out to be a pretty swell kid for Ken and Will and Juan-Carlos to play with. They never once stole any chilis or chased any grouses, and they still had fun.

Will did go back up to the Cross of the Martyrs, though, and sometimes Yoji went with him. Ken was Will's best friend, but there were times when Yoji was the one he needed to talk to.

"You think the world'll ever be the same again?" Will said one afternoon as they were looking down at it.

"Never," Yoji said.

Will looked at him closely. There was no hate, no anger in his eyes.

"You don't think that's bad?" Will said. "That the world will never be the same?"

"I used to. Now I think different sometimes means better."

"What made you change your mind?" Will said.

"A hakujin I know," Yoji said.

He slanted his eyes down at Will, and he smiled.

Will clasped his hands in his lap. *Keep building up, Dad,* he thought as he looked down at them. *'Cause that's what God's got me doin' here.*

FOCUS ON THE FAMILY®

Like this book?

Then you'll love *Clubhouse* magazine! It's written for kids just like you, and it's loaded with great stories, interesting articles, puzzles, games, and fun things for you to do. Some issues include posters, too! With your parents' permission, we'll even send you a complimentary copy.

Simply write to Focus on the Family, Colorado Springs, CO 80995 (in Canada, write P.O. 9800, Stn. Terminal, Vancouver, B.C. V6B 4G3) and mention that you saw this offer in the back of this book. Or, call 1-800-A-FAMILY (in Canada, call 1-800-661-9800).

You may also visit our Web site (www.family.org) to learn more about the ministry or find out if there is a Focus on the Family office in your country.

● ● ●

"Adventures in Odyssey" is a fantastic series of books, videos, and radio dramas that's fun for the entire family—parents, too! You'll love the twists and turns found in the novels, as well as the excitement packed into every video. And the 30 albums of radio dramas (available on audiocassette or compact disc) are great to listen to in the car, after dinner . . . even at bedtime! You can hear "Adventures in Odyssey" on the radio, too. Call Focus on the Family for a listing of local stations airing these programs or to request any of the "Adventures in Odyssey" resources. They're also available at Christian bookstores everywhere.

Focus on the Family is an organization that is dedicated to helping you and your family establish lasting, loving relationships with each other and the Lord. It's why we exist! If we can assist you or your family in any way, please feel free to contact us. We'd love to hear from you!

More Great Resources
From Focus on the Family ®

KidWitness Tales

New from Heritage Builders, a ministry of Focus on the Family, these action-packed tales follow fictional Bible-era kids who meet real Bible characters from the Old and New Testaments. Recommended for ages 8 and up.

The Worst Wish

Seth, the son of Jairus, thinks his sister, Tabitha, is the biggest pest! She won't leave him and his friends alone. She tattles on them and makes them look bad when they memorize Scripture. Seth's friends finally give him an ultimatum: prove to us that we're more important to you than your sister or that's the end of the friendship. Seth wishes his sister would die, but when she does, he is devastated. He knows her death is all his fault! As he pours out his sorrow to God, he realizes the importance of family relationships.

Trouble Times Ten

Ben is afraid of almost everything—especially water. Now, Israel is rejoicing in the appearance of Moses, who has said he will free them from Egypt. But instead of freedom, plague after plague comes to the land, intensifying Ben's fears. When Israel is finally released, Ben discovers he must pass through two walls of water. Just as he makes it through, he sees a child who is in danger of drowning. Ben realizes it's time to face his fear of water and learn to trust God.

Ruled Out

Ethan is tired of rules. Not only must he follow his father's strict household rules and the rules about Passover and manna—but now Moses is going up to Mount Sinai to get even more rules from God! To make things worse, Ethan's sister, Leah, loves rules and keeps track of who follows them. Ethan, tired of being taunted by rebellious kids for following the rules, joins their mischief. While he has fun for a while, he later feels guilty for what he's done. He learns the hard way that rules are there for his protection.

Crazy Jacob

Andrew and his dad, Jacob, have always enjoyed a strong relationship. But lately, Jacob's been acting strange—talking to himself, staying out all night among caves and tombs, even becoming violent at times. Known now as "Crazy Jacob," the Gadarene demoniac, the townspeople have found it necessary to chain him up. When Andrew meets Jesus, he hopes He'll have the answer. But Andrew learns lessons about sacrificing what he wants before receiving the blessing he so desperately craves.

Galen and Goliath

Kids ages 8 and up will enjoy this lively tale about Galen, a 10-year-old, orphaned Philistine boy seeking Goliath's approval. The life lessons and values in this story will resonate with young readers, who will relate to Galen's yearning to be recognized by Goliath as a strong, real man. He thinks that brave acts will win him this respect; but through a string of unexpected events, Galen learns God's truth: Real men gain honor and respect not by bullying others, but by honoring and serving God.

Dangerous Dreams

The world teaches us its definition of success and freedom, but the reality is that they are only found in God. Kids ages 8 and up will get wrapped up in the adventurous story of strong-hearted Livy, the slave of Procula, the wife of Pontius Pilate. As Livy plots her escape, unexpected events cause her to question what exactly she is searching for. Jesus' answer is a far cry from the world's. Discover, through the magic of a fictional story, the abundant love and life that is found in Christ!

● ● ●

Look for these special books in your Christian bookstore or request a copy by calling 1-800-A-FAMILY (1-800-232-6459). Friends in Canada may write to Focus on the Family, P.O. Box 9800, Stn. Terminal, Vancouver, B.C. V6B 4G3 or call 1-800-661-9800.

Visit our Web site (www.family.org) to learn more about the ministry or to find out if there is a Focus on the Family office in your country.